Mandy Rose
and the
Secret
of a Lifetime

Hannah N. Fossette

First published by Hannah N. Fossette in 2024
Copyright © Hannah N. Fossette, 2024

This novel is a work of fiction. Names, characters, and incidents are either the product of the author's imagination or are used fictitiously, and any resemblance to actual persons, living or dead, events or localities is entirely coincidental.

For permission contact:
hannahssouthernbelledesigns@gmail.com
Cover Design By: Hannah N. Fossette
First edition

For my sweet cousin, Elle
who loves mermaids, after pandas

Chapter One

"Amanda, sweetie," my mom said as she knelt down in front of me all dressed up for a night out with my dad. Her blonde hair was curled and hung down around her head, while her blue eyes stood out against the gold eyeshadow that matched her dress. "We'll be back after you are in bed, so we will see you tomorrow morning, ok?"

I nodded my head and let my dirty blonde hair fall free and partly cover my face. I didn't like it when mom and dad were gone during my bedtime. I just wanted them to tuck me in and read me bedtime stories like they normally do because my babysitter never does anything like my parents do. She makes sure that I've brushed my teeth and gotten into bed and then leaves me to go do who knows what while I lay in bed and try to fall asleep.

I watched as Dad knelt down beside Mom and tried to get me to look him in the eye. I didn't want to look him in the eye and kept my head down; however, Dad put his hand underneath my chin and gently lifted my head. He searched my eyes silently without saying anything. I wanted to pull away, but Dad's strong hand kept me there, which meant I had no choice but to stare back into his blue eyes, which were exactly like mine. As I stood there, I realized that his usual messy hair was actually styled, which meant he was serious about this night out with Mom. "Be good for Miss Charlotte. I know you don't like it when we aren't here to put you to bed, but Mommy and Daddy have to go out tonight. Can you promise me you'll be good?"

I stayed silent for a moment debating if I should promise Dad or throw a tantrum like other kids my age, but I eventually made up my mind. "I promise, Daddy." I didn't want to promise him, but I also wanted to be a good girl for my parents. I just didn't want them to leave.

"That's my girl," Dad said as he pulled me into a hug. "Love you, kiddo."

"Love you, too," I responded with a small sniffle.

Mom kissed me on the forehead. "You'll be ok, sweetie. You're going to have a lot of fun with Miss Charlotte, and we'll be back before you even know it!" Mom said as she stood up from kneeling. "Love you, sweetie."

"Love you too, Mommy."

I stood there watching as Mom and Dad gave last-minute instructions to Miss Charlotte before they went out for the night, and I couldn't help but feel sad as I watched them go. I wanted to be put to bed and tucked in by Mom and Dad because I already knew that Miss Charlotte would never tuck me in no matter how much I begged for it. I mean isn't that normal for a five-year-old to want to be tucked in by their mom and dad? What kid wouldn't want to be?

As soon as the front door closed, I ran to the window hoping my parents would change their minds, but sadly they didn't. I watched dejectedly as my parents got into their car, leaving me behind. Just before they drove away, they did wave goodbye to me; however, it didn't make me feel better.

Miss Charlotte approached me carefully and knelt down beside me, "Amanda, how about I go make us some dinner?"

"Ok," I replied without looking away from the window.

I heard Miss Charlotte sigh. "I know you miss your parents and would rather have them here with you than me, but I promise that we will have fun together." She held her hand out to me. "Let's go to the kitchen and decide what we should have for dinner. We could even play a game to decide what we eat."

At the mention of a game, I perked up a little bit. "Ok! Let's go then!" I cried, pulling Miss Charlotte as fast as I could to the kitchen. I always love playing games, and I even forgot to miss my parents for a short period of time. Well, until later that night.

Chapter Two

I spent the night playing games, such as hide-n-seek and tag, with Miss Charlotte and had completely forgotten to miss my parents until Miss Charlotte decided that she was too tired to keep going and went to the guest room to lay down for a bit, leaving me to fend for myself.

After Miss Charlotte had retired to the guest room, the feeling of sadness returned. In an attempt to keep my mind off missing my parents, I decided to watch some TV.

I grabbed my favorite blanket from my room and tiptoed back downstairs to the couch, making sure I didn't wake up Miss Charlotte. Miss Charlotte is a good babysitter when she has energy, but when she is tired, it's hard to stay on her good side, which I found out the hard way the first time she babysat me. She may only be seventeen, but when she's in a bad mood, it's best to stay away and let her sleep it off.

I curled up on the couch settling in to watch one of the popular kids' movies that was playing, and it wasn't long before I had lost myself in the movie- that was until I started to feel hot… extremely hot.

For a second, I thought I had a fever and was coming down with a cold, but it didn't take long before I realized it wasn't just a cold. My skin had started to burn and itch, and I highly doubted it was normal for a cold.

The burning and itching started at my fingertips, but it soon began to travel up my arms and spread across my body. Everything was burning and itching.

I scratched my itching skin, hoping to ease the pain, but all it did was make my skin burn more.

"Miss Charlotte!" I screamed hoping to wake her up. I didn't want to get into trouble, but I was also really scared and didn't care at the moment. "Miss Charlotte, please help me!"

She didn't seem to hear me, and the burning was only getting worse. My breathing was becoming ragged, and my vision was beginning to fade.

I whimpered from the pain. Miss Charlotte couldn't hear me, and no one else was around to hear me. There aren't even any neighbors to hear me scream. My parents and I live on top of a hill with our nearest neighbor on the edge of the bustling town below.

I laid there, curled up on the couch, accepting my fate, until I remembered what Mom would do to help me whenever I had a fever. She would put a cold damp cloth on my head to help ease the pain, which gave me an idea.

With my vision fading in and out, I stumbled to the kitchen in a last attempt to stop the burning and itching. I turned on some cold water in the sink and splashed it onto my face. After the first splash of cold water, my burning and itching skin calmed down just a tiny bit, but it was just enough to give me some relief.

That tiny bit of relief gave me a new resolve to keep going. With each splash of cold water, I could feel my skin and body calming down, going back to normal, which gave me such sweet relief. My vision also stopped fading in and out.

At last, everything was back to normal. I turned off the running water, dried my face with the kitchen towel, and slid down against the cabinets to the floor. I sat there taking slow, deep breaths, calming my racing heart.

"That was terrifying," I muttered to myself. "I don't ever want to feel like that again."

Little did I know that my moment of sweet utter relief would only last a few short moments.

My hands started burning again, and I groaned inwardly. I didn't want to have to go through all of that again!

Instead of running cold water on my hands like before, I decided to go ahead and wake up Miss Charlotte, even if it meant she got upset at me. However, at that particular moment, I really didn't care. I just wanted to stop hurting.

Standing up from the floor, I made my way back through the family room to the stairs, but before I even started climbing, I noticed that there was an odd pink glow coming from somewhere below me. Curious, I looked down and realized that the pink light was coming from my hands!

I immediately screamed and backed into a wall, staring wide eyed at my glowing hands. What in the world was going on with me?

Completely terrified, I watched as pink magic shot

out of my hands. It went in every direction, destroying everything in sight.

"No! This can't be happening. What do I do? How do I stop it?" I cried, desperately hoping Mom and Dad would walk in right now and help me out.

If I didn't do something quickly, the whole house was going to be completely destroyed, but I didn't know what to do! I racked my brain for a solution and ended up just sticking my hands in my pockets.

Almost immediately, everything stopped. My hands stopped burning and glowing, and nothing was being destroyed. However, there was a huge mess of broken furniture and fallen pieces from the walls and ceiling.

For a second, all I did was stare at the huge mess I had created. How was I going to explain all of this to Miss Charlotte, let alone my parents, and how was I going to explain that I had magic?

Then suddenly, an idea came to mind. If I could destroy all of this, couldn't I fix it, too?

Renewed by this new thought, I carefully lifted my hands out of my pockets, but nothing happened.

"Why isn't it working?" I whispered to myself. "What do I need to do to get it to work?"

In movies, it always seemed so simple. It would just work automatically. What was I missing to be able to activate my magic?

The sound of the TV crackling diverted my attention away from the mess for a second, and I realized that amidst all the damage, the TV had hardly been touched, which was very surprising. I watched as the staticky screen came back to life and played the movie I was watching earlier.

"*To be able to master the skill of art, you must be able to imagine what you want to draw before drawing it,*" stated the main character's art teacher from the movie. *"The only thing stopping you is your imagination. Your imagination is endless, but you have to want it to draw it. It's not because you can't do it."*

Although it's just a movie, what the art teacher said gave me an idea. Maybe the reason why I couldn't use my magic was because I wasn't imagining what I wanted to do.

Taking a slow deep breath, I imagined what the destroyed furniture and walls looked like before. Slowly but surely my hands started turning pink again. At first, it wasn't very bright, but as I kept imagining the details of the furniture and walls, the magic burned brighter.

Finally, the magic smoothly sailed out of my hands to the mess, fixing what was broken. I watched in complete awe as the pile of debris fixed itself, leaving behind only what was there before.

I sighed in relief as I sat down on the floor overjoyed that I wouldn't get in trouble for breaking my parents' things.

As soon as the shock of what happened settled in, I quickly realized that I did indeed have another problem. I somehow had magic, and I didn't know where it came from or why I had it, but thankfully, at least, everything was fixed. I was also grateful that Miss Charlotte didn't wake up. She probably would've lost it if she saw what happened, but thank goodness, she's a heavy sleeper!

I was completely exhausted from the night's adventure, so I headed upstairs to my room for the night with a strange feeling in my mind. It kind of felt like I was afraid for some reason, and I wasn't sure why. The strange feeling made me think that I couldn't let anyone know I had magic. It was just an overwhelming feeling that it wasn't safe for others to know about this strange magic

I had. I didn't even feel like it was safe enough to tell my parents.

As I laid down on my bed, I looked at my hands and muttered, "I must keep this a secret. I can't let anyone know about this, not even my parents."

Chapter Three

The ocean breeze was nice as I strolled along the shoreline, careful not to get in the water. It had been a long first day at school, and I was grateful for a couple moments to myself before I had to go home to do my homework and chores.

Although school had started once again, the beach was full of parents with their kids and teenagers hanging out. It was like a normal hot summer day and not like the first day of school, but then again, as long as it's nice out, the beach is almost always filled with people enjoying it.

I stopped my walk to watch some high school seniors setting up the usual spot for a bonfire later that night. Each year the seniors get together on the night of the first and last day of school to celebrate making it this far.

It's always a fun event to watch. In past years, there have been marshmallow roastings, a volleyball tournament for those who want to participate, and the fun tradition of whose sandcastle is the best with the principal and his wife as the judges. This year I finally get to join in on the festivities.

I was finally a senior in high school, and I couldn't wait for tonight. I've always watched the seniors with great anticipation of the day I would get my chance. I didn't want to bother the seniors setting up, so I continued my walk determined to finish my homework and chores, that way I could enjoy the party tonight.

Continuing on, I passed more families and friends enjoying their time on the beach and in the ocean. It was relaxing to see everyone having fun. I even watched a little girl run in front of me, squealing with excitement all the way to the ocean.

I always wondered what it would be like to go into the ocean, but sadly, my parents have forbidden me from going into any kind of body of water, including the ocean and pool. They are terrified of any kind of water that can submerge you fully or even partially, which is the vast majority of bodies of water, including baths.

I don't even get to enjoy baths. I'm only allowed to take showers. I guess they just have a fear of drowning, but I'm not really sure. I've never asked why.

Before I walked much farther, I heard a woman shriek. "Please, help! My baby is drowning!" the woman yelled.

Turning around, I saw the little girl from earlier struggling to keep her head above the waves with no one being close enough to grab her. Even her own mother was too far up the beach to get to her in time. I was the only one close enough to grab her, but that would mean breaking my parents' rule.

I only had a split second to make my decision. I could've used my magic, but others would have seen it. That would've caused too many questions, and I wasn't even sure if I could control it enough to not hurt someone. It may have been twelve years of having magic, but that doesn't mean I've been able to practice it. Too many prying eyes could find out.

Making my decision, I took off sprinting for the little girl, praying that I'd get to her in time before she drowns. I hesitated as my feet hit the ocean wondering if breaking my parents' rule was indeed a good idea, but seeing the terrified look on the girl's face was all I needed to step in farther.

"Hold on! I'm coming!" I yelled to the terrified girl as I waded farther into the ocean.

I struggled through the waves myself as I got closer to where the girl was. I wasn't used to having to fight waves, and I'm sure people could tell.

The water was up to my waist. My legs didn't exactly feel right, but I didn't dwell on it because I was finally within reach of the girl.

Right before I could grab ahold of her, she slipped below the surface of the water leaving behind a trail of bubbles.

"No!" I screamed and immediately sank below the surface to find her.

Opening my eyes in the salty water burned my eyes, but I was determined to save her. I saw her holding her breath and flailing just out of my reach. I tried moving my legs, but they felt stuck together and weren't moving, which sent fear into me, but I couldn't let that stop me now. I was so close.

The only thing I could do now was use my magic. I didn't want to, but it was the only option left, and hopefully no one would see a pink glow come from underneath the ocean.

I quickly focused and imagined a small current that

would push her closer to me. As my hands turned pink, I hoped that nothing would happen, since I hadn't really used my magic much, but thankfully, the little girl floated closer to me without any complications.

I quickly grabbed the girl and straightened my legs. We breached the surface as soon as I thought my lungs were going to explode, and I'm sure the girl felt the same way.

It was such a sweet relief as air filled my lungs again. I took a couple deep breaths steadying my pounding heart before I took a good look at the girl.

She was conscious and breathing, but she looked completely petrified. She clung to me as hard as she could, and I couldn't even blame her after what she just went through.

"Are you alright?" I asked, holding her close to hopefully give her some kind of comfort. She simply nodded her head and gripped my shirt tighter.

"Ok, then, let's get you back to your mother."

I tried to move, but my legs felt stiffer than before. I couldn't move them apart from each other, and they felt weird. I couldn't comprehend what it felt like, but I didn't think it was normal for that to happen.

Panic surged through me. If I couldn't move, how was I supposed to get back to the shore with the little girl?

Chapter Four

I couldn't move my legs, and my heart started to race. I tried my hardest to keep a level head so I wouldn't scare the girl, but it was getting harder with each second that passed.

The people on the shore were cheering that I had saved the girl, but they didn't know I couldn't move and bring her there. The stiffness was almost up to my waist. I feared what would happen if it spread to the rest of my body.

Too many people were watching. I couldn't use magic once again. What could I do?

If I couldn't separate my legs, maybe I could bend my legs and jump, I thought. I struggled to bend my legs, but it did work.

I pushed off the seafloor and jumped. It was just a little jump, but it was enough to give me some confidence in making it out alive.

My legs felt numb and weak, but I kept jumping. I couldn't give up now when we were so close.

After jumping for what felt like ages, we were almost to the shore. The water was only up to my knees now, and I could feel my legs slowly returning to normal.

I could barely separate my legs, but it calmed my racing heart to know that my legs did, in fact, still work. Walking was much faster than jumping, and I made faster time.

As soon as I stepped out of the water, the girl's mother and a group of people who had gathered came swarming up to me.

The girl's mother got to me the fastest and held out her arms for her little girl, and I gladly gave the frightened girl back to her joyful mother.

"Oh, my precious baby! I'm so happy you are safe!" the girl's mother cried, hugging and soothing her child. "Thank you so much for saving my daughter. How could I ever repay you?"

I smiled. It felt good to have been able to save a life, even if it was terrifying in the moment. "Of course, I'm happy I was able to get to her in time. I'm sure anyone here would have done the same thing."

"But still, there must be something I can do for you. You saved my precious Savannah, after all."

"Oh, no, it's completely fine," I reassured her, shaking my head.

I heard her sigh. "If you insist. Well, if you ever need anything, feel free to come find me, and I'll see if I can help. I'm Sadie Pritchet, by the way."

"Amanda. Nice to meet you, but I should get going. I do hope that Savannah isn't hurt."

"Nice to meet you, too, and thank you."

As soon as I was out of sight of everyone and there

was no one around, I collapsed onto the sand from exhaustion. I laid there on the warm sand, trying to regain my breath and calm my nerves.

What I felt out there could not have been normal. There's no way it could've been, but if it's not normal, then what was that feeling?

Maybe I could find out if I went back into the ocean. I know it's a very dumb idea, but my curiosity was getting the better of me. Anyway, if something happens, I could use my magic. There wasn't anyone around to see if I did use it.

Cautiously, I entered the ocean again. One step at a time, I slowly worked my way into deeper waters and stopped once it was up to my waist, since last time it started there, too.

For a second, nothing happened, and I thought it was all just my imagination. However, as soon as I thought my legs weren't going to become stiff, it started.

This time it didn't take long for my legs to become stiff and feel stuck together. Once again, I couldn't move, and fear set in quickly.

Why did I want to come out here again? Why did I let my curiosity get the better of me? I should've just stayed on the sand and forgotten about it!

As soon as it had started, I suddenly felt a peaceful calm come over me. It was like I was meant to be out in the ocean. It felt so invigorating. Well, that is, until I slipped under the surface.

This time I flailed my arms around, like the little girl did earlier, trying to get back up because my legs weren't working, and I didn't know how to swim.

In a desperate attempt to get back above the water before my lungs gave out, I opened my eyes, but this time they didn't burn, which was very surprising until I saw something that was even more shocking. My legs had completely disappeared and were replaced by a tail. It wasn't just any old tail; it looked like a mermaid tail!

I screamed. Regretting that decision immediately, I covered my mouth with my hand. Because of the foolish scream I just let out, the air in my lungs was disappearing fast, and I still couldn't get up to the surface. Not only could I not get back above the surface, but the current was also slowly pulling me out to sea. Surely this is where I die.

Then a thought ran through my mind. Mermaids breathe underwater, duh. It was either hold my breath and die or try to breathe and possibly die from sucking in water. I went with the chance of living.

I slowly breathed out and breathed in. As I was breathing in, I waited for water to come pouring into my mouth, but it never came, which was when I realized that I could, indeed, breathe underwater!

Just as the sweet relief set in that I wasn't going to die, questions came pouring into my mind. How was this possible? How did I turn into a mermaid? Will I be able to change back into a human, or will I stay a mermaid forever?

That last question sent a bolt of fear into my heart. If I couldn't change back into a human, I would never see my parents again, nor would I ever be able to walk and run again.

Maybe if I could get the water to go below my waist, maybe, just maybe, I would turn back. It was my best option, but first, I had to learn how to swim.

First things first, I faced the direction of land and flicked my tail. I moved just a little bit. I'm sure I did not look graceful at all, but I was swimming. With every flick of my tail, I grew closer to land.

Thankfully, when I got to shallow water and the water stayed off the majority of my tail, it slowly started to turn back into legs. It was a weird sensation, but at least, I didn't have to worry about never being a human again.

For a second, I laid on the sand with the waves gently rolling over my legs. "Do Mom and Dad know about this? Is that why I've never been allowed in water?" I asked myself. "If so, why didn't they want me to know? Why would they keep this from me?"

I sighed. I couldn't let my parents know about this either. I now not only have one secret but two to keep from them.

I know I shouldn't keep my magic and becoming a mermaid from my parents, but if I told them, it would lead to way too many questions. Not to mention they would find out that I broke their rule of going into the ocean, which would get me into deep trouble I didn't want. So, I guess for now, I'll have to keep these secrets.

Chapter Five

Six o' clock on Monday morning, I was getting ready for school when my mom yelled for me.

"Yes?" I yelled back.

"Come here, please!"

"Coming!" I ran down the stairs into the family room to find my mom standing there, and I was afraid I had done something. Did I accidentally destroy something in my sleep with my magic? "What did you need?"

"I need you to go to the fabric store and buy a box of thread." Phew, thankfully, I didn't destroy anything. I was worried since I've woken up a couple times to find that something in my room had been destroyed, and I haven't figured out how to stop my magic when I'm asleep.

"Yes, ma'am," I replied and hurried off to the nearest fabric store without asking what kind. I didn't have much time before I had to leave for school, so I had to be quick.

In my haste to get to the store quickly, I accidentally ran into someone and fell to the ground. "Oh no! I'm so sorry! I wasn't paying attention and didn't see you. It's my fault."

"Hello, Amanda," the person I ran into said, and I immediately recognized their voice.

"Oh, hello, Mr. Sniper. I'm sorry I ran into you," I said, standing up from the ground.

Mr. Sniper is the owner of a bait and tackle shop. He lives alone, and I don't think he has much of a life. Although he has helped me out a couple of times, he does kind of freak me out, but he also always seems to be sad. It's almost like he is lost in thought all the time. I'm not sure, but maybe he lost someone close to him a while ago, and that's why he always seems to be sad. I don't know, but that's my best guess. His smile is gentle looking, but everyone fears him because he keeps to himself- at least, we kids do. It also doesn't help that he has piercing blue eyes and very blonde hair, which can be very intimidating at times.

"No harm done. What are you doing out here so early?" he asked, breaking into my thoughts.

"Oh, just getting something for my mom. I-I'd better get going." I rushed off before he could reply, but I could feel him staring after me, which made my hair stand up on the back of my neck.

When I finally got to Mrs. June's Fashion Boutique, I was out of breath from running the whole way there. Although it was downhill on the way here, it took a lot of energy trying to keep from falling, and I have to go uphill to get back home, which is going to be tough with being out of breath and energy.

"Hello, Amanda. How can I help you today? Maybe

some fabric for a new outfit? Or maybe even a new outfit tailored to fit?" Mrs. June asked enthusiastically.

Even though I was in a hurry, I felt bad interrupting Mrs. June. She is a sweet, lovely, little old lady, who enjoys opening up her boutique early in the morning to catch people who need to pick up something before they go to work or school. Exactly how you would imagine her, she is petite and ever so kind. Mrs. June has white hair neatly arranged in a bun and blue eyes. Everyone loves her. She's like the perfect grandma you could imagine. Although she isn't my grandmother, Mrs. June has taken care of me whenever I was upset when I was younger. Even now, she looks after me whenever I come to get fabric and stuff for my mom.

"I need to buy a box of thread, please," I answered.

"Any specific color you need or one of each color?"

"Umm, one of each color, please." I wasn't sure what my mom needed because I forgot to ask before I left, but it was too late now. I also forgot my phone, so I couldn't even call her.

"Okay, dear, that will be thirteen dollars." I paid Mrs. June, thanked her, and bolted out of the store.

Gasping for air, I sprinted down the street knowing I was going to be late for school, and I breathed a sigh of relief when my house came into sight.

My legs and lungs were burning when I entered the house, but I found Mom waiting in the hallway by the stairs. Thankfully, I managed to make it over to her even though my legs felt like jelly. I handed Mom her box of thread and headed for my room.

"Amanda, you got the wrong box of thread," Mom said as I was walking upstairs.

I mentally slapped myself for the mistake. "I'm sorry, Mom. I forgot to ask, and I left my phone here."

She sighed, and I could see the turmoil in her eyes, trying to figure out what to do. "It's alright, but you will have a list of chores you need to do after you get home from school for forgetting to ask which thread and for leaving your phone. If something had happened, I wouldn't have been able to get a hold of you, and you wouldn't have been able to reach me or your father."

"I understand, but after I finish cleaning, will it still be ok if I go out?"

"Yes, you may go out after you are done with your chores." After Mom left, I continued to walk upstairs to finish getting ready and grab my backpack and phone.

Because I was in a regular t-shirt and shorts, I put on a maroon t-shirt with a tie in front, blue jeans, and white tennis shoes. To complete my outfit, I wore a white watch with gold trimming. It was a simple yet cute outfit, and I kept my wavy hair natural.

Just as I was grabbing my backpack and phone, I happened to glance at my alarm clock. If I didn't leave now, I was going to be late for school!

I practically ran down the steps into the kitchen. "Bye Mom. Bye Dad," I said hurriedly as I grabbed an apple from the fruit basket since I didn't have time to eat an actual breakfast.

"Amanda, are you not going to eat anything?" Mom asked. "I made breakfast for you."

"I'm sorry, Mom. I don't have time today. I'm going to be late."

Once again, I heard her sigh. I felt awful for making my mom sad, but I really didn't have time. Instead, I crossed over to where she was standing and gave her a hug. "I really am sorry, Mom. I'm sure it's delicious. I just don't have time today."

"I understand, sweetie. Maybe next time," she said as

she kissed me on the head. "Run along now. You don't want to be late. Love you."

Dad looked up from his newspaper where he sat at the kitchen table. "Love you, kiddo. Have a good day at school."

"Love you both!" I called out to my parents as I sprinted for the door.

Because I wasn't allowed to ride the bus, and I didn't have a car even though I have a license, I had to walk to school, which was pretty far from my house. I was going to be lucky if I made it to school on time. Letting out a sigh, I asked the worst possible question. Can things get any worse? It turns out that it can.

Chapter Six

I made it with some time to spare, and I thought I was in the clear until I ran into Becky Southerland, the last person I wanted to see right now. Becky is the school bully, and everyone that isn't in her group of minions tries to stay out of her way. Her very dark brown hair that almost looks black and piercing green eyes are sure to make you want to stay out of her way. Her skin is also tan all the time. I don't know how she does it, but it seriously looks like she has a beach tan all year long!

"Well, look what the tide has brought in. It's the freak," Becky sneered at me.

"Please leave me alone, Becky. I'm not in the mood for you right now." I wanted to walk away, but with her glaring at me, I thought better of it and stayed put. At times like these, I wished her twin brother Anthony, who is also my boyfriend, was here. Anthony looks exactly like Becky, just the guy version, but he does not act like her at all. He's actually kind to everyone he meets and does not have a problem with me unlike his sister.

"Well, someone's upset today, I see. What should I do to you for talking back?" One of Becky's minions immediately grabbed my hair as Becky stalked closer to me.

This wasn't good. Everyone that was within hearing distance was looking at us. Some pitied me, while others were curious to see what Becky would do to me. I desperately wanted out of this situation.

Without thinking of a better idea, I grabbed my hair out of Becky's minion's grasp, yelled, "Just leave me alone," and ran off to the bathroom to calm down.

As I was running away, I heard collective gasps and Becky yelling after me, "You'll regret this!"

I paced back and forth in the bathroom, hoping that I didn't look as rattled on the outside as I felt on the inside. I couldn't keep letting Becky get to me, but she's hated me since we were in kindergarten. It's been a lifetime of her hating me for I don't even know why, and I highly doubt that I could change that.

Shortly after calming down, I looked at my phone and realized that if I didn't go to homeroom now, I was going to be late. Miss Fox, my homeroom teacher, is famous for sending students to detention for being late. Not only did I not want detention, but Becky and her minions are also in my homeroom. I didn't want to give them any more ammunition to use against me.

As soon as I walked into class, the bell rang signaling the start of classes. "Miss Rose, so happy you could join us," Miss Fox stated.

"I'm sorry, Miss Fox. It won't happen again."

I could hear Becky and her minions snickering as I went to my seat, but I also heard Miss Fox sigh. "It is alright, Amanda. I will excuse you for being almost late today- only because your friend Anthony came by earlier and told me that something had come up and that you might be a little late." My mouth fell open. How did Anthony know what happened, and how did he convince Miss Fox to pardon me? That rarely ever happens! "Now, I want everyone to finish up their homework or study. I do not want to hear a word out of anyone unless it is to ask a question," threatened Miss Fox.

"Yes, ma'am," everyone replied as we all pulled out our books, and I made a mental note to thank Anthony later for his help.

After that whole ordeal, everything went smoothly until lunch. I went to sit as far away as I could get from everyone like I usually do, when out of nowhere came Becky's foot.

I couldn't react fast enough and face-planted on the floor. There was a sickening thud as my head collided with the tile of the cafeteria floor, which was cold and hard.

Becky leaned down and whispered, "Next time, watch what you say; otherwise, you won't be let off as easily next time."

Shortly after sitting down, Anthony joined me. "Hi, Mandy, are you ok? I'm so sorry that Becky keeps bullying you."

"I'm ok, and don't worry about it. It's not like I'm not used to it."

"I know, but I really hoped that she would stop bullying people by now, especially you."

I felt my cheeks heat up slightly, but I laughed it off. "She has hated me for years; I highly doubt that she will change, especially after yelling at her this morning."

"Oh, yeah, speaking of this morning. I saw what happened, so I got Miss Fox to pardon you by volunteering to pick up trash Saturday around town."

"Thank you for getting Miss Fox to pardon me, but you

didn't have to do that!"

"It's only one day. Besides, I wanted to do something to help my girlfriend get out of trouble. Anyways, want to come join me at the jocks' table?"

I sighed. I wasn't sure if his friends would want me to sit with them, but I didn't want to sit alone either. "Um, sure, I'll join you and your friends."

His face lit up with the biggest smile I have ever seen from him. "Really? Are you sure? I don't want to pressure you."

I smiled. It was nice of him to be worried about me. "I'm sure."

His friends didn't mind that I joined them, and I actually had fun talking to them. It felt great being able to talk to some other people, and I even got to talk to some girls whose boyfriends were at the table. It was a little awkward at first, but it was a great first step into making more friends, since all my previous friends dropped me for Becky as soon as we reached high school. It's fine though. Anthony's been there for me, which has helped.

As soon as school finished, I headed home and got to work doing the chores my parents had written down for me to do, and in no time, I finished. I started to go to my room but then realized that I wanted to see my best friends, who are real live mermaids, which certainly helps with the fact that my previous human friends didn't want to hang out with me anymore because who wouldn't want mermaids as best friends?

I met my best friends shortly after finding out that I was a half-mermaid.

I had gone exploring and pulled myself onto a small island. As I watched my sparkly pink tail disappear, I heard a soft "Oh" and a splash. I looked into the water and found mermaids, but they quickly swam away. Determined not to lose them, I went after them.

"Please wait! I don't want to hurt you. I just want to talk to you, please!" They turned around, and every single one of their mouths gaped open in shock.

The mermaid with wavy, auburn hair and a turquoise tail recovered first. "Hi, I'm Coral Cove, and these are my friends Sirena and Isla Ray, and Melody Song." The other mermaids were still in shock but managed a small wave as a hello. Sirena and Isla, who must've been twins, both had sparkling red tails and straight, black hair, but Sirena had purple highlights, while Isla had blue. Melody had wavy, black hair and a sparkly green tail.

I waved back at them. "It's nice to meet you all. I'm Amanda Rose, but you can call me Mandy for short. It's so cool to meet other mermaids! I thought I was the only one!" Anthony is the only one who still calls me Mandy, since my nickname is more for my friends to use, so I thought it would be pretty neat if mermaids used my nickname as well.

"How in the oceans did you change into a mermaid? I have never seen a human turn into a mermaid before!"

"Is it witchcraft?" exclaimed Sirena and Isla.

I suddenly realized that they might discover my magic and that this might have been a bad idea. Before I could think of a way out, Melody spoke up from where she was treading water. "It's not witchcraft. She's a half-mermaid." She was soft-spoken, but her beauty made her stand out more than the others.

"Half-mermaid?" I asked.

"A half-mermaid is a human on land and a mermaid in water."

"Oh!" Sirena gasped. "That's right! I completely forgot that we studied half-mermaids last semester! How could

I have forgotten that? I am so sorry if we offended you, Mandy!"

"It's alright. I didn't even know that half-mermaids and mermaids existed until a couple of hours ago."

"Hope you don't mind me asking, but wouldn't you know about mermaids and half-mermaids? Aren't one of your parents a mermaid or merman?"

I was taken back by that question, but I quickly recovered. "Not that I know of unless one is a half-mermaid. They hate the ocean, though, so I doubt I will ever know. Not to mention, I can't exactly ask them about it since I'm not supposed to be here."

"Hmm, maybe they just don't want you to know about merpeople. It's not exactly safe for half-mermaids to exist," Coral stated but quickly covered her mouth with her hand. "Sorry, I shouldn't have told you that. I didn't mean to scare you. It's just complicated."

"It's ok, but why is it dangerous?"

The four of them looked at each other, but only Melody spoke this time. "We probably shouldn't tell you that. We can get into trouble if this gets out, but as long as no one says anything, it should be ok."

"That doesn't mean we can't continue meeting each other though!" Coral quickly added. "It would be so cool to have a half-mermaid as a friend!"

I couldn't help but laugh. Coral's enthusiasm was contagious as smiles broke out on everyone's faces. "Ok, that sounds good! It's so cool that I get to have mermaids as friends! I just thought mermaids were something out of a fairytale!"

Melody smiled. "Not everything is a fairytale."

"I can see that now." I looked up at the sky and realized that the sun was beginning to set. "I am so sorry to cut this short, but I have to get home. I've been out here longer than I thought! It was nice getting to meet you all!"

"It was nice getting to meet you, too!" everyone exclaimed.

"If you want, you can come back to this spot. We hang out around these rocks a lot to study, since it's away from the other mergirls and merboys," Isla mentioned.

"Sounds good! I hope I get to see you all soon!" I said as I waved goodbye and headed back to shore, but I did have to wonder if either my mom or dad is a half-mermaid.

Ever since then, which has been a couple weeks, I have been sneaking out to meet them, and we've all become best friends. I just can't let my parents find out, since that would lead to more trouble.

Chapter Seven

Making my decision, I quickly turned around and went back downstairs. "Hey, Dad, is it ok if I go to the beach? I got all my chores done." I crossed my fingers, hoping he wouldn't say no.

"I guess you can since you finished, but why do you want to go to the beach? Is it because of Anthony?"

"Kind of. Anthony is at the gym with his friends right now. He said that if they got out in time, he would meet me at the pier, and we could hang out together. I was just going to walk on the beach until he hopefully gets there." The good thing is that we did plan to meet each other later, but the bad thing is I wasn't technically going to wait for him on the beach. I didn't want to lie to him, but I couldn't exactly tell him either, which made it harder.

"Alright, be careful then and be back before curfew. Have fun, and don't go in the ocean!"

"Ok, thank you!" I wish I didn't have to go against

my parents' rule, but I knew that if I told them, I would never see my friends again.

I quickly made my way down the hill our house was located on to get to the beach, which isn't far from the bottom. Once I stepped onto the beach, I walked down to one of the lesser used piers. That way, I wouldn't be spotted when my tail appears.

Standing on the sand underneath the pier, I glanced around quickly to ensure no one was watching and slipped into the water.

As soon as my tail appeared, I swam as fast as possible to the island. Technically, we didn't plan to meet today, but I hoped they would be there to study. Once I got there, I saw them sitting on the sand with their seaweed scrolls, and I was relieved to find them there.

"Hi, girls!" I called out to them as I waved and immediately swam up to them.

There were some surprised looks as I swam up to them. They were definitely confused about why I was able to be there since I usually don't hang out with them on school nights unless we already had plans.

"Mandy! What are you doing here on a school night? Did we have plans that I forgot about?"

"Isla!" Sirena scolded.

Before Sirena could scold her sister more, Coral quickly cut in, "I believe what she meant to say is we are delighted to see you. We were just a little surprised since it was a school night. Right, Isla?"

"Yeah, that's what I meant. Sorry."

"No worries. I'm sorry to drop by without there being plans; I just needed a little escape until I meet up with my boyfriend later."

"You are always welcome to drop by, Mandy!" Sirena exclaimed.

"Yeah, just because we don't have plans doesn't mean you can't visit us. You can sit here with us if you want. We can make room, so you fit." Melody patted the sand beside her.

"Oh, it's ok. I don't need to sit. I can just lay on the sand in the water, but thank you." I kind of felt weird letting them see me in human form. I know they are ok with it, but I just don't want to freak them out.

"Is everything ok, Mandy?" Coral asked. "You mentioned earlier that you needed an escape. Did something happen?"

"Oh, yeah, it was just a rough day, but it's better now that I am here with y'all! Anyways, what are you guys studying?" I asked, quickly changing the subject. I shouldn't worry them about my problems with Becky and my old friends.

"We've been studying a chapter on haunted places in Surviving the Oceans. It's fascinating!" answered Sirena. "There is even-"

"There's a haunted cave near here!"

"Isla! Stop interrupting me!" Sirena yelled while lunging at Isla, which made them fall into the ocean.

As the twins were fighting each other, Melody spoke up, "According to our scrolls, there is indeed a haunted cave near here called Moon Bay Cave. Although it is supposedly haunted, it also says that there is a hidden waterfall in the cave. The waterfall is supposed to hold a magical element that cures all kinds of pains and sicknesses, but of course, that is only a legend since only a few merpeople have made it back outside the cave alive."

"Well, that sounds fun," I said sarcastically, nearly rolling my eyes.

"We should go check it out!" Isla exclaimed. I glanced

at the others, and we all kind of looked at each other, like is she insane? "Oh, come on! It can't hurt to check it out!"

"I guess it wouldn't," Coral said thoughtfully. "Is everyone up for it?" Some of us were reluctant, but we all said yes.

"I guess we are going to the cave then," I said even though I wasn't sure if that was a good idea or not. Checking out a spooky cave that not a lot of merpeople have come back out of didn't exactly sound pleasant.

Chapter Eight

The girls packed up their seaweed scrolls and put them in their bags to get ready for the swim to Moon Bay Cave.

"Alright, let's get going! This is gonna be so much fun!" Isla exclaimed.

"If you say so," I responded.

"Haha, hopefully we survive this. I'm not sure this is a great idea, Isla," said Melody.

Although Melody was the only one to voice her concern, all of us were thinking the same thing except for perhaps Isla who seemed more thrilled with every passing second.

"It will be fun. I promise!" exclaimed Isla.

She seemed so enthusiastic that nothing could go wrong. Meanwhile, I could think of a bunch of different ways this could go wrong. "So, why is the cave haunted?" I asked.

"Oh, it's haunted because supposedly an evil merman

shows up whenever someone enters the cave, and very few merfolk make it back out alive," answered Sirena. "As well as there being an evil merman, King Neptune tried to make it to the waterfall to see if the legends were true or not, but he never reached it."

Coral spoke up and added, "According to what our seaweed scrolls said, King Neptune barely made it out alive. It says that the only reason he was able to was because of the powers in the golden trident he carries around."

"If he didn't have the trident with him at that time, he would have been another victim that the cave has claimed. Ever since his near-death experience with the cave, hardly any merpeople dare to enter it for fear that they, too, will become a victim," continued Melody. "But I'm sure everything will be fine. I hope."

"This just keeps getting better and better, doesn't it," I mumbled. Just the fact that many merpeople have died in that cave was enough to make me turn back around and say forget it, but I had already said that I would go with them. I couldn't back down now. It was too late.

"I know, right! Isn't it so exciting! We could be the first mermaids to reach the waterfall and prove if it has magical healing powers or not!" exclaimed Isla as she swam ahead of everyone else.

I rolled my eyes. How could she be excited about going into a cave that could kill us? "Is she always like this?" I asked Sirena.

"Pretty much. She hardly ever backs down in the face of danger."

"I'm not sure if that's a good thing or not."

"Oh, it will come back to bite her one day. I'm sure of that. I just don't know when, but don't worry. I doubt the cave is really haunted. It's just a merbaby tale we tell the little ones so that they behave. We may or may not threaten them that we will take them to the cave and have the evil merman take them."

"How about we change the subject?" Melody asked.

"That sounds great." This was the perfect chance for me to find out more about Neptune. "What is King Neptune like, anyways? I've heard fairy tales about him on land, but I doubt they are completely truthful."

Melody's eyes lit up. "Some of what humans know is partly true, but the stories have gotten distorted throughout the years." I could tell that Melody likes facts and history. Every time she starts talking about them, she becomes as excited as a kid in a candy store- maybe even more excited. "As you know, King Neptune is known as the King of the Seas. That part is definitely true, but the tales of his power differ among who tells you. Even we do not know his full capabilities, but what we do know is that the power comes from the golden trident he holds, which has been passed down through the generations of queens and kings."

"However, we do know that his capabilities have at least power over the oceans and wind," said Coral. "Other than that, we can only guess what powers he has from merfolk tales passed down to us. If you want, we can share some of our favorite stories with you."

I was really interested to hear what his powers might be. Maybe hearing about them would help me with my own magic. "I would love to hear about them. Anything to keep my mind off the deadly cave we are heading to." Everyone laughed nervously at that. Even though we all said yes, only Isla really seemed to want to go.

This time Isla jumped in. "My favorite story is that King Neptune can turn merpeople to stone and curse them! Legends say that it has only happened a couple times, and he only uses those powers when absolutely necessary. It is also said that the merpeople who were turned to stone still stand in his coral garden. We don't know why they were turned to stone, but I bet it was because they double-crossed him in some way." At this, she looked positively excited that there might be stone merpeople somewhere out there living as nothing but decoration in the King's garden.

"I am slightly concerned about her." Isla can scare me at times whenever she talks about things like that. She lights up when something spooky is mentioned and doesn't calm down for quite a while. It's like she thrives on it.

"We all are," confirmed Coral. "She's been excited about spooky things for as long as I've known her, which is pretty much our whole lives. Anyways, my favorite legend is that he can create anything he wants. I've been told that he has created multiple places that are absolutely beautiful! Islands, castles, and lagoons are just some of the places he has supposedly created, but they are all hidden. I really do hope this legend is true though! Can you just imagine how gorgeous it would be?"

"I agree with Coral. The legend that he can create beautiful places is enough to make any mermaid happy!" exclaimed Sirena as she and Coral pretended to faint.

I had to laugh. Both Sirena and Coral could be extra at times, but I guess it goes well with the stories of mermaids on land. "What's yours, Melody?"

"Hmm, I would have to say mine is that he knows who the next ruler will be when the heir is born before anyone else. It could be anyone who is the next heir, even if they are not born into the royal family. It's been said that the King of the Seas will only step down once the next rightful king or queen has become of age, even if it's been hundreds of years since they took the throne. I believe this to be true because the ages of past kings and queens all vary drastically. Some are younger and some are older when they step down from the throne."

"That's true. I've never thought of that before," stated Coral. "I wonder how past kings and queens knew about the next heir when the heir wasn't in their family."

Before Coral could say anything else, Isla exclaimed, "We're here!"

The cave looked like an ordinary cave. It didn't seem like it was haunted, but suddenly, I had a horrible sick feeling crash through me. It was like my insides were twisting against each other, and I felt sick. For some reason, even though I have never seen this cave before, it felt like I had.

Chapter Nine

The gut feeling that I had seen Moon Bay Cave before continued to grow as we swam closer to the entrance, but I couldn't explain it. There was no way that I had ever seen the cave before.

"Mandy, are you ok?" asked Sirena. "You are looking a little pale."

"Hmm? Oh, yeah, I'm fine." I'm probably just scared since I have never done something like this before. It's nothing I needed to worry the girls with. "Is everyone ready to head inside?"

"I was born ready!" Isla exclaimed as everyone else nodded their heads.

As soon as we entered the cave, the atmosphere around us seemed to change. It felt colder. It was almost like someone was watching us, which sent chills running down my back.

The water was slightly lit up with a soft blue glow,

which definitely made it seem spookier, and apparently, I wasn't the only one who thought so, too. "Why is the water glowing like this?" Isla asked with her voice shaking. For the first time since we got here, Isla seemed to be scared.

"I'm not completely sure, but the glowing might be from bioluminescent plankton living in the water. I guess this is the reason why they call the cave Moon Bay Cave," stated Melody.

"It sure does make the cave spookier."

"Yes, but it also makes it look beautiful!" exclaimed Coral. "It really does make it seem like the moon is shining down on the water." Coral was right. It did make the cave look like we were under the night sky. If we weren't in a cave that could kill us at any moment, I would have found it quite beautiful and relaxing.

We continued to swim through the various tunnels looking for the waterfall, but we were all huddled together as close as we could get without swimming into one another.

The farther we swam, the more confused I was about where we came from. There were so many tunnels, and none of them showed any signs that we were getting closer to the waterfall or back to the entrance of the cave. To make matters worse, every single tunnel looked exactly the same!

"Does anyone know where the entrance is?" I asked. "I'm beginning to think that we might be lost." I started shaking. I'm not sure if it was because the water was cold or if it was because of fear, but either way I was really beginning to regret letting them take me here. I should have listened to that gut feeling and asked them to not go in. They may have thought of me as a scaredy cat, but at least, we would be safe!

Sirena spoke up, "I'm afraid I don't know."

"Me neither," Coral stated.

"I was keeping track of the turns, but we've taken so many that I lost track. I'm afraid that we might indeed be lost," stated Melody with a hint of fear in her voice.

Isla wrapped her arms around herself. "Does that mean we are trapped here?" Her bravado act had completely diminished. She now looked like a terrified child who had lost her mom.

"It doesn't mean we are trapped here forever. I just don't know where we came from. How about we keep swimming and see if we can find anything familiar."

We continued swimming, but you could feel the fear radiating from each of us. This was no longer a game of finding the waterfall; it was a game of surviving.

It was completely silent as we kept swimming, but all of a sudden, I happened to hear a noise. It sounded like something was hitting the water. "Girls, I hear something. Listen."

All of us stopped and listened to what now sounded like liquid hitting the water we were in. "It's the waterfall. It has to be!" exclaimed Coral.

We swam around another corner and found the waterfall lit up by the bioluminescence plankton. It wasn't very big and loud, but the waterfall flowed down the cave wall into the water below like something out of a dream.

"It's beautiful," Isla said in awe.

The waterfall was mesmerizing to watch, but Sirena spoke up and asked, "Now that we are here, how are we going to test if it can heal us?"

"Good question, Sirena," Melody stated. "Maybe we could-"

Right as Melody was suggesting what we could do,

the water we were in started to swirl around us. The swirling water whipped us around like we were inside of a whirlpool.

I called out to the others, "What's going on?"

"I don't know," replied Sirena. "I can't see anything!"

The rapidly spinning water made it increasingly hard to see anything. Every so often I could see someone's hair fly in front of my face, but other than that, I couldn't see anything but bubbles.

Without warning, the water stopped. We were all lying on the seafloor dizzy from our sudden encounter.

I brushed the sand off my tail. "Well, that was fun. Can't say I want to do that again." I looked up into my friends' faces and saw that all of them were as white as ghosts. They were looking at something behind me. "What's wrong?" I asked scared to find out what was behind me.

I turned around to find a merman staring at us. He looked evil. He had a dark green, shark-like tail, fiery red hair, and piercing black eyes. He locked eyes with me, and I could've sworn I heard a small chuckle as he flashed a crooked grin at me.

His hands turned red, and the next thing I knew, a ball of red magic was sailing towards us. He was aiming to kill us or at least hurt us.

I didn't have time to think of the consequences of using my magic. I jumped in front of my friends and willed myself to create a shield strong enough to block the attack.

Just as his ball of magic would have ended us, a pink, sparkly shield of magic appeared around us. As soon as his ball of magic hit my shield, it exploded sending the evil merman flipping backwards into the cave wall.

My friends were still in shock, so I grabbed them

using my magic and swam as fast as I could out of there. I turned down multiple tunnels, each one the same as the last, but eventually, I found the exit. The fear I felt must've helped me navigate the tunnels, which I am very grateful for.

I pulled all my friends to safety outside the cave into the open water, but I didn't stop there. I continued to swim, pulling them along behind me, all the way to the island where we hang out. I was afraid that if we stopped, the merman would find us. If that happened, I wasn't sure if I could hold him off again, so it was safer this way.

I looked back at where we came from. Thankfully, the merman didn't follow us, but I now had the problem that my friends knew about my magic. Whether I liked it or not, I was going to have to answer their questions, which meant I would have to tell them my secret.

Chapter Ten

I sat on the sand of the island as I waited for my friends to come out of their shock.

Because I was too far out of the water, my tail had disappeared, but this time, I didn't care if I freaked my friends out with my legs. I just wanted to be out of the water.

One by one, they came out of their shock and sat in silence staring at me. I shifted my sitting position. I felt like I was on trial for something out of my control.

Isla spoke first, "How did you do that? Are you seriously using witchcraft?"

"Isla, be nice. I'm sure there is a reasonable explanation, right, Mandy?" asked Melody as she eyed me suspiciously.

"I, um, I don't really know how to explain it." I never thought my secret would get out like this. How was I supposed to explain my magic when I don't even know why I have it!

"How about you start at the beginning."

"Um, ok, but I don't really know much about it either. My magic just suddenly showed up when I was five, and I'm not completely sure how I got it." I explained to them everything I knew, which wasn't much. I also explained to them that I seem to be able to use my magic when I envision it. It just doesn't seem to happen on its own.

When I finished explaining, I couldn't look them in the eyes. I had kept a major secret from them, and I doubted that they would want to continue being friends with me after this. I was a half-mermaid freak with magic. Why would they want to be friends with me?

Coral spoke softly. "Mandy, why didn't you tell us sooner?"

"I haven't had anyone to tell before because I was afraid people would start using me for my magic and that I might be put into danger. I'm a total freak, aren't I? I understand if you all don't want to be my friends anymore."

"What?" Sirena asked. "You aren't a freak, why would you think that we don't want to be friends with you anymore?"

"Well, I'm a half-mermaid with magical powers. Isn't that enough to call me a freak?"

"No, it doesn't make you a freak, Mandy," stated Coral. "It makes you an incredible merperson. Right, girls?"

"Right!" they replied.

"Mandy, I'm sorry that I accused you of using witchcraft again," Isla said guiltily. "I just didn't realize that there might be a different reason why you have magic."

"It's ok. I probably would've done the same thing if I were you."

"Now that everything is settled and that we are still friends, we have something to give you," said Sirena. She reached into her bag and pulled out a bracelet. "Here, this is for you. It's a friendship bracelet."

Curious, I took the bracelet and looked at it. The bracelet was made of white pearls with a blue pearl in the middle, and it sparkled in the sun. "It's beautiful!" I exclaimed. "Thank you!"

The girls smiled at me as Melody spoke up. "It's a friendship bracelet, and each of us have one." They all showed their bracelets on their wrists. I don't know why I didn't see them earlier.

"They are all beautiful! Thank you again!" As I slipped my bracelet onto my wrist I happened to glance at my waterproof watch. "I'm sorry, girls, but I need to go. I didn't realize the time. I'm going to be late to meet up with Anthony!"

"Ooh, have fun with your boyfriend!" Coral exclaimed while the other girls laughed at her reaction. Sometimes Coral acted like the stereotype humans think mermaids are more than I think Coral realizes.

"Bye! I'll see you all again Saturday!" I called as they all echoed their own goodbyes before swimming off to their own homes.

As I was swimming back to the shore, I noticed dark clouds covering the sky, which wasn't a good sign. By the looks of it, it looked like a powerful storm was coming in.

When I was a little ways off from the shore, the wind started to pick up creating bigger waves, and rain started to pour down on me. Great, hanging out with Anthony was going to be harder now, but at least I would have an excuse for why I was soaked.

I arrived at the shore under the pier, and thankfully, no

one was there since it was raining. I quickly grabbed my phone from a little compartment in a rock and headed to the pizzeria on top of the pier where I was supposed to meet Anthony.

No sooner had I opened the door, I saw Anthony sitting at a booth up against the windows facing the ocean, and I quickly walked over to him and sat across from him.

Thankfully, because of the storm, you couldn't see the ocean that well, which meant that Anthony wouldn't have seen me in the ocean and how I transformed back into a human.

"Hi, Anthony. I'm sorry if I kept you waiting long. I kind of lost track of time."

"No worries. I figured you lost track of time or something like that," he said as he laughed. "It seems to be a regular occurrence with you." His smile told me that he was joking, but I still felt bad for making him wait. "Anyway, I did go ahead and order a cheese pizza for us. Mr. Giovanni said that he would bring it out once he saw that you were here."

"Sounds good. What did you want to do today? I guess we can't do anything outside because of the storm."

"Yeah, that's a bummer. I was hoping that we could play volleyball on the beach, but I guess that's not going to happen now."

He looked so sad that his plans got ruined by the rain, and I hoped that I could cheer him up. "Maybe we could go bowling instead? It's kind of like volleyball. Just, you know, with rolling a ball instead of hitting one."

His face immediately lit up, which gave me the satisfaction of knowing that I cheered him up, even if it was just a little. "That's a good idea! We haven't gone bowling in a while."

"Hello, Amanda. Good to see you again. It's been awhile since you two have been here to eat my pizza," Mr. Giovanni said as he brought over our cheese pizza.

"Oh, hello, Mr. Giovanni. It has been a while, hasn't it? It's good to see you, though." Mr. Giovanni is the owner of the best pizza place in town. Well, it is the only pizza place in town, but his pizza is still really good. He and his wife moved here from Italy years ago, and ever since then they have become an important part of the everyday lives of the Davenport townspeople. Mr. Giovanni always makes it a priority to talk to his customers, which has led to him becoming friends with basically everyone in town.

Mr. Giovanni smiled, "It's always a pleasure to see you two. Enjoy your pizza, and I hope to see you all again soon!"

"We'll come back again soon. Don't worry!" Anthony replied. "Now, let's eat. I'm starving!"

I laughed. "Aren't you always hungry?"

"Hey! Not all the time." Anthony smiled. "Just almost always."

We ate our cheese pizza, talking and laughing about what had happened at school and what he and his friends did at the gym. Apparently, one of his friends tried to jump over him, which didn't work, and they both went crashing to the ground. I couldn't help but laugh. It sounded like it looked ridiculous.

Once we had eaten our pizza, Anthony asked, "Shall we head to the bowling alley?"

"Sounds good to me."

"Alright let's go then!"

We cleared our dirty dishes and trash off the table and headed to the door where we ran into Mr. Sniper.

"Well, hello again, Amanda," said Mr. Sniper. "It's

good to see you again, and hello, Anthony."

We both replied in sync saying, "Hello, Mr. Sniper."

"Now where might you two be off to on this stormy night?"

"Oh, we were just on our way to the bowling alley, sir," Anthony replied.

"Well, don't let me stop you. I'm just here to pick up my pizza, but be careful both of you. Never know what this storm might bring."

"Yes sir, thank you, and you should be careful as well."

Mr. Sniper nodded his head, but he looked a little surprised to hear Anthony say that.

"Let's get going, Mandy," said Anthony as he put a hand on my back to guide me out the door. Normally that would've made my heart skip a beat, but it was overpowered by Mr. Sniper's intense gaze. "Have a good night, Mr. Sniper."

Anthony held the door open for me and led the way to his car as he breathed a sigh of relief. "Thank goodness we got to leave. He still scares me after all these years!"

"I know, right? I accidentally ran into him this morning, and even after I apologized, I could still feel him watching me as I walked away."

"Oh, so that's why you apologized."

"Yeah, I was hoping he wouldn't still be mad, but thankfully, it looked like he wasn't."

Anthony shrugged. "I'm sure he's gotten over it by now, but let's not dwell on it too much. We have a bowling night to get to!" He exclaimed as he punched the air.

I couldn't help but laugh. He's always excited when we get to hang out together, but he's always super excited when we get to play some sort of game, which I guess goes along well with him being a football player. I don't mind, though. I also enjoy playing games with him.

We are both very competitive, which always makes it interesting and fun.

The bowling alley was packed when we arrived, and Anthony was barely able to find a parking spot.

"It sure is busy tonight," said Anthony. "I wonder what's going on."

"I'm not sure. I didn't think this many people would be here on a Monday night."

As we were walking, the word Monday kept ringing in my ears as if I was supposed to know something, and right before we got to the door, it finally hit me. I facepalmed for forgetting.

"Whoa, you ok? What brought that on?" Anthony asked with concern.

"It's Monday night, which means it's bowling league night. I can't believe I forgot that!"

"Oh, I guess that makes sense, now."

We were now inside the bowling alley, and you could definitely tell that the bowling league was going on. It was really loud, and there were people everywhere.

"I'm so sorry, Anthony. I wouldn't have suggested this if I remembered. Now we may not even get to bowl." I was completely dejected. All I wanted to do was cheer him up since his idea didn't work, but all I did was suggest something else that wouldn't work.

"Hey, it's okay," he said, trying to calm me down. "I'm sure they still have some lanes that aren't being used for the league. We might have to wait a little longer, but it's no big deal."

"Are you sure?"

"I'm sure. Come on. Let's go see if we can get a lane," he said, as he grabbed my hand, pulling me through the crowd to the counter.

We did have to wait a little bit for a lane, but it didn't

take as long as I initially thought it would. As we were walking to our lane with our bowling shoes and balls, we passed by the Wrecking Balls, and I pulled Anthony to a stop.

"Just a second, Anthony. Can we watch them for just a moment, please?"

The Wrecking Balls was a team made up of Mrs. June, her husband Mr. Dan, Mr. and Mrs. Windward, and Mr. and Mrs. Crawford. Each member was an elder of the community, and all of them were beyond nice to everyone.

Mr. Dan is a sweet older gentleman who volunteers his time in different organizations such as at church and cleaning trash around town. Both Mrs. June and Mr. Dan always insist that everyone call them by their first names because they hate the formalities of being called by their last name. I'm not even sure anyone remembers what their last name is anymore.

Anyway, Mr. and Mrs. Windward used to work on a ship to catch different kinds of fish and shellfish for Mr. and Mrs. Crawford's seafood restaurant. Although the Windwards and the Crawfords are a little too old to do as much as they used to, both of them have kids and grandkids who help run the businesses. In fact, the Crawford's oldest granddaughter is engaged to the Windward's second grandson, and their wedding is planned for sometime early next year.

"Sure, I don't see why not."

We walked a little closer to the crowd watching the Wrecking Balls bowl. They always seemed to have a crowd whenever they bowl.

We watched as Mrs. Crawford bowled a strike. "Nice!" Anthony called out to her as I clapped.

"Oh, Anthony and Amanda! I didn't know y'all were

here!"

"We just got here. We were heading to our lane when Mandy noticed y'all were playing."

I chimed in, "It looks like y'all are doing well! I hope you all score high tonight."

"Well, thank you dearie. It is always appreciated, but with that said, I hope we are crushing it," she said with a wink. "Anyway, I won't keep y'all from your own bowling fun. Now shoo, go have fun!"

Both Anthony and I laughed a little. "Thank you, Mrs. Crawford!" I said as we headed further down to our lane.

When we got to our lane and put our shoes on, I saw Anthony rub his hands together, and I knew exactly what he was gonna say before he even said it.

"Now," Anthony said, still rubbing his hands together with a mischievous grin. "Are you ready to get beaten?"

I returned his mischievous grin. "Ha, in your wildest dreams! I'll be the one winning tonight!"

"If you say so."

"Just watch. I'll show you!"

I picked up my bowling ball and got ready to bowl my first throw. As soon as I let go of the ball, I knew it was a bad bowl, and sure enough, it was. It went straight into the gutter, and I could hear Anthony laughing behind me.

The next throw wasn't much better. I only knocked down one pin.

I turned around to see him doubled over laughing uncontrollably. "If that's the best you've got, I'm definitely going to win."

"That was just my warmup. I want to see you do better," I said as I plopped down on the chair beside him.

"Oh, that'll be easy," he replied as he stood up and patted me on the shoulder. "Just watch and learn."

The clatter of pins being knocked down told me he hit way more pins than one, and sure enough, it was a strike!

He turned around with a smug smile on his face. "See, that's how you do it."

"Oh, whatever," I said, as I rolled my eyes. Of course, he had to show me up, but hey, at least he wasn't trying to let me win on purpose.

We continued bowling and teasing each other until we had played three games. Anthony won the first game, and I won the second game. The third game was close, but Anthony ended up winning. I didn't mind though. I liked that Anthony didn't go easy on me.

"Tonight was fun, Mandy. You did a great job bowling, but not good enough to beat me." He stuck his tongue out at me, and I playfully shoved him.

"Whatever," I said as I rolled my eyes. I looked at the time on my phone and realized that I only had ten minutes left before curfew. "Oh no! I'm going to be late for curfew!"

"Wait, what? Is it that late already?" He also looked at the time and realized that it was ten minutes till ten. "Come on. I'll drive you back to your house as fast as I can. There's still a chance."

We ran outside to his car in the pouring rain. If I was lucky, he might get me back in time, but I highly doubted it. I was hardly ever that lucky.

Chapter Eleven

As soon as we got to Anthony's car, Anthony started it up and began driving as fast as the speed limit and rain would allow us.

"I'm so sorry that I kept you out this late!"

"It's not your fault; it's mine. I should've kept better track of time."

We rode in complete silence except for the wind and rain hitting the windshield. Anthony was focused on watching the road, while I was panicking about being late. I had already gotten into trouble once today. What were my parents going to say if I got into trouble again? With that thought, I started bouncing my leg.

Anthony glanced over at me and noticed me bouncing my leg. "Hey, it'll be ok. I'm sure they'll understand," he reassured me.

He must've picked up that I bounce my leg when I get nervous. "Hopefully," I replied, giving him a small smile as a thanks. I've never told him that I bounce my leg when I get nervous, but it was nice to see that he had picked up on it.

Shortly after, Anthony pulled up in front of my house, and I braced myself for what was to come. It was fifteen minutes past ten, which meant I was late. This couldn't end well.

The fear must have been written on my face because Anthony seemed to notice. "I'm sure they can't be too upset at you. I'll go with you to the door and try to help smooth things over with them, ok?"

"Thank you, but you really don't have to do that."

"It's the right thing to do." He unbuckled his seatbelt and got out of the car. "Come on. It will be ok."

We walked up to the front door, and as soon as I opened the door, my parents were on the other side with their arms crossed waiting for me. Their faces were a mix of concern and anger, and I couldn't tell which one they were feeling more.

"Ahem, young lady, where have you been?" asked Dad.

"I'm sorry I'm late. I lost track of time, and the rain slowed us down getting here." I was so embarrassed that Anthony was having to watch this. I wanted to hang my head, but I knew I shouldn't unless I wanted to make my parents more upset.

"What were you doing to lose track of time like this, may I ask?" Mom asked, eyeing us suspiciously.

This time Anthony spoke up. "Mr. and Mrs. Rose, I'm afraid that it is mainly my fault for getting Mandy back here late. We were bowling, and I asked her if we could play a third game for a tie breaker. If I hadn't asked her to play a third game, I would have gotten her home sooner."

"You are a brave young man to speak up, but Amanda, you will still be punished for being late, even though it may not have been totally your fault," stated Dad.

"However," Mom said, "since this is your first time getting back late, your punishment will not be too bad. Now, if you'll excuse us, Anthony, we must discuss Amanda's punishment."

"Of course, Mr. and Mrs. Rose. Again, I'm sorry for getting Mandy home late." Anthony turned and started to head back out the door. However, before he completely left, he turned around and gave me a little wave to say goodbye, and I waved back as I watched him drive off in the pouring rain.

"Alright," Mom said, bringing me back to the fact that I still didn't know my punishment. "You will be grounded until Saturday. You may only leave your room for basic necessities, like meals and school. Do I make myself clear?"

Being grounded for four days was better than I expected, and I would still be able to hang out with my friends on Saturday. "Yes, ma'am."

"Good. Now, hand me your phone and go on up to your room."

Once I got to my room, I headed over to my desk to start my homework. Although my house is on a hill, it's not too high, but I still have an amazing view of the beach and ocean from my window seat. My desk just partially overlooks the ocean because the window is located at an angle from it, but it's still nice to look out and see a little bit of the ocean.

Thankfully, I didn't have too much homework to complete. As soon as I finished my homework, I started to get ready for bed and noticed that I still had my friendship bracelet on.

I headed to my closet and pulled off a loose panel in the wall, which revealed my jewelry box. I know. It's a weird place for a jewelry box, but I feel like it's safer there in case anyone ever breaks into the house.

I opened the jewelry box and put my friendship bracelet next to my heart shaped key necklace. The necklace is one of my most prized possessions. I'm not sure who gave it to me, but I have had it for as long as I can remember. I'm also not sure why I treasure it so much. I kind of just have a feeling that it was given to me by someone special.

Once I closed my jewelry box, I noticed a pink box was behind my jewelry box. I picked it up and noticed it had a name tag that said 'Amanda Pearl Rose'. It was my name, but I didn't know who put it there.

For some reason, I had a feeling that it was important, but I was also terrified of opening it. It kind of felt like it held an important secret begging me to open it. Although I was scared of what was inside the box, I was curious to see what was inside.

Chapter Twelve

My curiosity was getting the better of me. I grabbed the box and settled down onto my window seat. Of course, I can't see the ocean at night, but it's still comforting to sit there knowing it's not too far away, and if it's completely silent, sometimes I can hear the faint sound of the waves crashing onto the beach, which makes sitting here quite peaceful at night.

I pulled the ribbon off the box and opened it. Inside, I found a letter addressed to me and some small trinkets.

Curious, I opened the envelope and pulled out the letter.

Dear Amanda,

I do not know a better way to tell you this, but the people you are living with are not your birth parents. I know that this must come as a surprise to you, and I am truly sorry that you had to find out this way. However, there was no other way that I could tell you.

I am your mother, Mary Rose, a human, and your father is Paul Rose, a merman. The people you are living with are half-mermaids who work for King Neptune and have been keeping an eye on you since you were a baby to make sure that you wouldn't find out about mermaids. We had to be taken away from you because King Neptune forbids marriages between merfolk and humans.

If you have not found out already, you are a half-mermaid as well, and you also have magical powers. Your magical powers were given to you by your father before we were taken away from you. Your father also gave you a key-shaped necklace to help channel your magic. If you ever find that your magic is out of control, either hold or wear that necklace, and it will help get your magic under control. The necklace acts as a balance to calm both you and your magic down; that way, it's usable.

I wish that I could tell you more, but I am afraid that I must go now. I believe you will turn out to be a wonderful girl, and I want you to remember that we will always love you.

With Love,
Your Birth Mother

P.S. Do not let the people taking care of you find this. If they find out that you know about mermaids, you will be in danger.

I couldn't believe it. I didn't know what to feel. My

heart felt heavy, and too many emotions rushed through me. How did I not know? The signs were all there with my parents- no Neptune's employees- not letting me go in the ocean, and them never once mentioning that I have magic. I should've known, but I didn't.

If this was all true, how am I supposed to face the coming days knowing that my parents are not my parents? Could I still treat them the same way; that way, they wouldn't know that I know? If not, would they really harm me for knowing?

It felt like everything I knew was crashing down around me. My life seemed like a lie- a nightmare come true.

In an attempt to calm myself down, I pulled out the trinkets that were in the box with the first item being a picture. The picture showed a woman, a merman, and a baby looking happy on the edge of the water, which must've been my real parents. The strange thing was that my real parents looked exactly like my fake parents, which really confused me. I wasn't sure why they both looked the same. However, they looked so happy, and it did look like they really loved me. I just kind of wished that I got to know them, but instead, here I am living whatever kind of life this is.

The next item I pulled out was a locket, which looked small and dainty. Although the locket didn't have anything inside, it did have small flowers on the outside.

The last trinket in the box was a snow globe. The snow globe had a princess figurine inside dressed for cold weather. Even though I shouldn't have played the music in case someone heard, I ended up playing it anyway. The way the "snow" fell inside the snow globe and the soft music that played, it reminded me of winter with the joy it brings.

I figured both the locket and snow globe were my mom's since they didn't look like they had been damaged by water, and I wondered what they meant to her since she had given them to me.

I did have to admit that I was a little concerned about how the box showed up behind the panel in my closet, but I didn't have much time to worry about it because I heard footsteps heading toward my room.

Immediately, I grabbed everything and shoved it underneath my bed. As soon as it was all hidden, I grabbed my book that I had left out on the window seat and propped myself up as if I was reading just as there was a knock on my door.

"Amanda, can I come in?" my mom asked.

"Sure."

The door opened, and Mom- or whoever she was- opened the door. "Did you finish your homework?"

"Yes, I just finished a little bit ago."

"I know you got grounded because of coming home late, but did you at least have fun on your date with Anthony?"

"Oh, yes, it was fun. Bowling was especially fun. I almost beat him!" I know she wasn't my real mom, but it was good to see that at least it looked like she cared about me. At least, I hoped she did.

"Haha, that's good. You've always loved competitions no matter what it is." I smiled and nodded my head enthusiastically. "Well, I'm glad you had fun, but you should probably start getting ready for bed. You've got another early morning tomorrow."

"Ok, good night, Mom."

"Good night, sweetie. Love you," she said as she kissed the top of my head, which almost brought tears to my eyes. Maybe she did care for me after all.

"Love you, too. Tell Dad I said that I love him, too."
Mom smiled. "I will."

As I got into bed, I wondered if she really did love me. I mean they had both been there for me my entire life, but do they tell me they love me because they have to keep up the act or because they do? I wasn't sure anymore, but I drifted off to sleep before I could dwell on it more.

Chapter 13

When I got up the next morning, it felt like I had hardly slept at all. I had tossed and turned all night with nightmares of "my parents" finding out about my secrets and being turned over to Neptune for him to torture me, which plagued my sleep.

Completely exhausted, I got ready for school and headed downstairs to grab breakfast before heading out, and I hoped that the walk to school would wake me up. However, it did not.

Somehow, I managed to get through the first half of the day all the way to lunch. I'm not sure how I did since I was in a daze the majority of the time from the events last night, but thankfully, I did.

Once I got to the cafeteria, I saw Anthony sitting with his friends at the jock table. Instantly, I felt a little better and headed over to sit next to him.

"Hi, Anthony," I said as I sat down. Once I was seated,

I noticed a look of concern on his face.

"Hi, Mandy. Is everything ok? I haven't been able to get ahold of you since last night. What did your parents say?" Oh, he was worried about what happened after he left last night.

"About that, I may or may not be grounded and had my phone taken away until Saturday."

"What!"

"Yeah, but it's ok. It was a better punishment than what I thought it would be, but that also means that we won't be able to hang out again until then."

"No need to be sorry. Nothing you can do about it. I guess we can hang out on Sunday then. I'm still volunteering on Saturday for cleanup around town."

"Oh, right, I forgot about that. Sunday should work then."

Anthony joined in on his friends' conversation about football practice later, while I ate in silence still pondering the major truth bomb about my parents. Would I have to live forever keeping all these secrets, or would I eventually be able to share them?

I felt a poke on my shoulder, which made me jump since I was lost in my thoughts. "Sorry," said Anthony. "I didn't mean to scare you. You weren't responding, and I wasn't sure how to get you to snap out of the daze you were in."

"It's ok. I just wasn't expecting it. That's all." I noticed that it was just me and Anthony at the table. "Where'd everyone go?"

"They all left to get to their next class since lunch is almost over. That's why I was trying to get your attention. I didn't want to leave you, and you miss class."

"Oh, thank you. I wouldn't have noticed if you didn't say anything."

"No problem, but are you really ok? It's not like you to space out for that long. You just don't seem like yourself today."

It was nice of him to be concerned. I really wanted to tell him I wasn't alright, but that would mean telling him my secrets, which I couldn't do.

"Yes, I'm fine. I just have a lot on my mind today." I picked up my backpack from the floor. "We should probably get to class. If I don't see you again today, I'll see you tomorrow."

He didn't look too convinced that I was fine, so I managed a small smile. He studied me for a second, but eventually just sighed. "If you say so then, have a good rest of your day, and I'll see you."

Outside the cafeteria, we parted ways. We went to separate classes, and I hoped that all these secrets I was keeping from him did not get in the way of our relationship.

Chapter Fourteen

Slowly the days went by. It felt like it was taking forever for Saturday to come, but it did eventually come. I was finally free from being grounded, and I could go see my best friends.

Not only did I just want to see them, but I also wanted to tell them about the letter and have them answer a very important question about illegal marriages between humans and merpeople.

I quickly got dressed and put on a raincoat because it was still pouring outside. Ever since we found that evil looking merman in Moon Bay Cave, the storms haven't let up, which is making me wonder if he has something to do with them, but I didn't have time to ponder on it. The sooner I got to them, the sooner I could tell them about everything that happened.

After I put on my raincoat, I grabbed a waterproof bag to put my letter in so that it wouldn't get damaged in the rain or ocean, but before I could put it in the raincoat, I had to shrink it down with my magic. Otherwise, I wouldn't have been able to hide it in my raincoat.

Once the letter was hidden safely in my raincoat, I headed downstairs to make sure that I could leave the house.

"Hi, Mom. I am allowed to leave the house now, right?"

"Yes, you are allowed to leave the house now, but what are you going to do in the rain anyway?" she asked.

Before I had the chance to answer, my dad cut in, "If you are hanging out with Anthony, please keep track of the time this time. We don't want another repeat of Monday night, do we?"

"I promise that I will keep track of time, but I won't be with Anthony. He's helping clean up trash around town today. I will go see him briefly, but I will be spending the day with some friends instead."

"Alright, be careful and have fun then, Amanda," Mom said.

"I will. Bye," I called to them as I walked out the door.

Walking in the rain proved to be difficult. The wind had picked up considerably throughout the week, and I had to have my hair tied back into a bun to keep it from slapping me in the face. I had no idea how Anthony and the other volunteers were going to be able to do anything in the wind and rain.

I continued to walk through the pouring rain and raging wind until I got to Davenport's City Hall. Davenport is our town name. It's not a very big town, but it's still a decent size for a town near the beach.

Thankfully, the volunteers led by Miss Fox hadn't started yet, and I found Anthony on the city hall steps waiting for instructions.

As I got closer to him, he smiled and waved at me. "Hi, Mandy! Finally free from being grounded?"

"Yes, I am, thankfully." Before I could say anything else, a gust of wind went by nearly knocking us off our feet. "Yikes, how are you guys going to clean up trash in this weather?"

"Good question. I don't know. Hopefully, at least the wind dies down some, but I highly doubt that."

"Volunteers!" Miss Fox called over the wind. "It's time to get started. Please come on over here."

"Guess that's my cue. See you tomorrow."

"See you." I watched him head over to Miss Fox and silently prayed that no one would get hurt with the wind being as rough as it is. After I watched Anthony walk away, I made my journey back to the beach and slipped into the ocean.

The water wasn't much better than it was on land. The water was freezing, and the wind made giant waves that crashed down on top of me.

By the time I reached the island, I was completely out of breath. I had also swallowed way too much sea water and was coughing and gasping for air when I pulled myself out of the ocean.

"Mandy!" Sirena exclaimed.

"Are you ok?" Melody asked.

"I'll be fine in a second. Just exhausted," I said as I laid there on the sand trying to catch my breath.

"I bet," stated Isla. "It's pretty rough out there."

"Once you catch your breath, how about we go to my house?" asked Coral. "It won't be quite so windy, and we can escape the waves and rain as well."

"That sounds good," I replied.

"Great!"

"If we swim close to the ocean floor, it should be easier to swim," stated Melody. "Have you caught your breath enough to swim again?"

I nodded my head. "I should be ok." Truthfully, I still didn't catch my breath, but I wanted to get out of the storm as badly as the girls did.

"Ok, follow me then, girls," stated Coral as she dove into the water with the rest of us close behind.

It took my tail a second to appear, but after it had formed, I joined them at the ocean's floor. "You were right, Melody. Swimming close to the seafloor is definitely easier," I stated.

"Common sense really. We don't have to deal with the wind and waves as much."

We swam mostly in silence, and not long after, we passed a rock that had "Welcome to Seadeep" carved on it. I guess Seadeep is the name of the town. Honestly, it's smart to have it carved into the rock. That way, if humans ever found it, they would probably think that a human was playing around and carved the rock for fun.

We passed several merpeople as we swam through the town. Many mermaids and mermen were working, while mergirls and merboys were playing with each other. Some had balls made of seaweed, and others had toys made from things found in shipwrecks.

"We're here," Coral said. She had stopped in front of her house, which was made out of coral and rocks. It was pretty ingenious if you asked me, but it didn't look that big. "Come on inside. My parents are out working right now, but we can hang out in my room."

Coral swam over to one side of her house, moved a rock, and swam down into a tunnel.

Curious, I swam after her into the tunnel and ended up in Coral's room.

"That's so cool!" I exclaimed as I exited the tunnel. I would've never thought of mermaids using tunnels underground to stay out of sight of humans. No wonder humans have never found solid proof of mermaids existing.

"Isn't it?" Sirena said as she swam into the room after me. "Because of humans, we can't build big houses on top of the sea floor, so instead, we build under them."

"It's pretty cool that you all have figured out how to build these."

When Isla swam into the room, she asked, "What should we do since we can't do anything outside?"

I wanted to tell them about the letter, but I figured it wasn't the right time. Everyone seemed to be happy at the moment, and I didn't want to spoil their weekend yet because of my own problems.

For a moment, no one seemed to have any suggestions until Coral spoke up. "How about we give each other makeovers?" she asked. "I've got plenty of supplies that we can use."

"Oh, yes!" Sirena exclaimed. "That seems like a great idea. It would be so much fun!"

Everyone seemed super excited, but I wasn't really sure what they were going to use that wouldn't wash away in the water. Then suddenly, they all turned towards me with a hint of glee in their eyes, which kind of scared me. "What?" I asked.

"This will be your first makeover as a mermaid!" Coral exclaimed.

Oh no. Correction, I was really scared. They looked like a pack of ravenous animals ready to prey on me, which certainly couldn't end well.

"Don't look so scared." Melody stated. "It's going to be fun."

"Uh-huh, if you say so." I've never had a makeover on land let alone underwater, and I wasn't sure how well this was going to end. It could be really good, or really bad.

Chapter Fifteen

Immediately, they all swam towards me, ecstatic to get started on my makeover, and I questioned my decision to come today.

"Hmm, what should we make her look like?" Isla asked. "Maybe we can go for a goth or spooky look?"

"Nah, that wouldn't look good on her," Sirena stated matter of fact.

"Ooh, I know!" exclaimed Melody. "We could make her look like a sorceress since she has magic."

"Yes, yes!" cried Sirena.

"That would be perfect," said Coral as she chimed in. "What do you think, Mandy? Should we make you look like a sorceress?"

"Um, I guess. I'm kind of new at the whole makeover thing, so just do whatever you all think is best."

"Perfect then. Let's get started!"

"First things first. Let's get that jacket off you. That

way, nothing will be in the way." stated Melody.

After Melody pulled my raincoat off, it was just a blur of events as they all rushed around getting supplies to transform me into a sorceress. Sirena pulled my hair out of the bun I had it in and started brushing it, while Coral grabbed jars where I assumed her makeup was stored to start on my face. Melody grabbed stuff to work on my tail, and Isla looked through Coral's closet for clothing ideas.

In between Coral applying makeup to my face, I saw Melody applying a green goo that was sticky to my tail in patterns. "Melody, what's that stuff you are applying to my tail? Do I even want to know?"

"Oh, this is sea slug slime. We use it as an adhesive to things. In this case, I'm using it to stick red colored sand to your tail to make swirling patterns."

"That's interesting." I wasn't too sure if I liked the idea of sea slug slime being on my tail, but I couldn't spoil their fun with the makeover, so I let it slide this time.

Anyway, I am always learning something new. I guess sea slug slime is like glue for mermaids, which is pretty ingenious.

Coral spoke up, "It's really hard to get sea slug slime though because it's not an easy process to extract it from the sea slugs. It's not exactly rare though. Now, stop moving, so I don't mess up your makeup."

"Sorry."

"Hey, Coral," Sirena said. "Where's your hair accessories?"

"Top right drawer on my vanity."

"Ah, found it. Thanks."

"No problem."

It wasn't even a couple seconds later that I heard Isla cry, "I found it! I found the perfect outfit!"

"Great! Now, Mandy, go put this on behind the curtain over there, and we'll get to see how you look!" Isla said as she handed me the outfit and pushed me toward the curtain.

"Ok," I replied, swimming behind the curtain, taking the outfit with me.

The outfit Isla had given me was a reddish, orangish crop top with one thick strap and one skinny strap, and it looked like it would cut off right above my stomach. She had also given me what looked like a matching flowing skirt to go over my tail.

Because I haven't really seen mermaids wear a skirt over their tails, I didn't know they had things like this because whenever my tail appears my shorts, jeans, whatever I'm wearing on my legs disappear until my legs come back. I still had so much to learn about mermaids, and I thought that I had already learned a lot.

After changing, I swam back out from behind the curtain, uncertain of how I looked. I was both excited and nervous, since I've never done something like this before, but I did hope that I looked good considering how hard they worked. At least for their sake, I hoped it turned out okay. "What do you think?"

Their eyes lit up. "You look gorgeous!" Sirena cried.

"As pretty as a princess!" exclaimed Coral.

Sirena pulled me over to Coral's full-length mirror, which I am assuming she had gotten from a shipwreck or something. "Now, what do you think? Do you like it?"

I looked at my reflection, and honestly, I was surprised at what I saw. My hair flowed behind me with little pearls placed in it, and my tail looked gorgeous with the red spirals Melody had drawn on it. I was amazed that I looked like a sorceress, and I wasn't even sure that my reflection was me.

"Wow, you all did a wonderful job! I can hardly tell that's me in there!"

"So, you like it?" asked Sirena with a hopeful look in her eyes.

"Like it? I love it! Thank you all so much! I can't believe you girls were able to make me look like this!"

"Well, we all had to make sure you had a great first mermaid makeover, didn't we, girls?" Coral asked.

I could see in the mirror that they were all smiling and nodding their heads, and I felt overjoyed that they were my friends. It almost even brought tears to my eyes. They are such great friends. I don't know what I did to deserve them.

I turned around smiling. "Who's next?"

Chapter Sixteen

We set to work giving the rest of them makeovers. Although it was fun, I couldn't help it and think of my problems at times, but I would quickly push them aside and continue having fun with my friends.

By the time we finished giving each other makeovers, Isla looked like a ghost, Melody was a teacher, and both Coral and Sirena looked like princesses.

"You all look great!" I said enthusiastically. It was really fun giving them makeovers, and it did help keep my mind off things. Who knew it would be this fun to hang out with mermaids?

Coral laughed. "Thank you, Mandy. It was a lot of fun."

"Now that we've all given each other makeovers, how about you tell us what's bothering you, Mandy," stated Melody.

"Wait, how'd you all know something was wrong?" I asked. I thought I hid it pretty well, but I guess I didn't.

"You just don't seem as enthusiastic today like normal. You seem a little down today."

"Yeah, so spill it," demanded Isla. "And we won't let you go until you tell us."

Sirena coughed. "What she means to say is, we hope you tell us what's bothering you, but if you don't want to tell us, we understand. Just know that we are here for you if you need us."

For a moment, I definitely wanted to back out of telling them about my parents. I didn't want to tell them this way. I didn't think they'd figure out that something was wrong, and most of all I certainly didn't want them to pity me.

However, I searched their eyes, and I got the feeling that maybe, just maybe, they'd help me out instead of taking pity on me.

Finally, I conceded with a sigh. "It would probably be better to show you guys." I swam over to Coral's bed where my raincoat had been laid and pulled out the waterproof bag containing the letter, careful to make sure that the letter hadn't been ruined. Swimming back over to Coral, unshrinking it as I went, I let her hold it. "Here, this will explain it."

The other girls looked over Coral's shoulders as they read the letter. I tried to read their expressions, but they managed to keep a straight face, which meant I had no clue what they were thinking.

I fidgeted with my hair while I waited for them to finish. With each passing second, my anxiety grew worse, afraid of what they would say.

Finally, after what felt like a lifetime, they all looked up with tears in their eyes.

"Oh, my goodness, Mandy," Coral said quietly. "Are you ok? That was a lot to take in all at once."

"I'm sure I'll be ok, eventually. It just might take me a while to get used to the fact that I guess I'll probably never get to meet my real parents."

"Well, we are all here for you if you ever need anything," Melody stated. "Even if it is just someone to talk to." Everyone nodded their heads in agreement.

"Thank you, girls. I appreciate it, and there is one thing I'd like to know though. Why are marriages between merfolk and humans illegal, and why could it be dangerous for me?"

The girls shifted uncomfortably. "Um, I'm not sure if we should tell you," Isla said.

"Please," I begged. "I need to know why my real parents were taken away from me."

Melody looked at my pleading eyes and sighed. "We should tell her. She does have a right to know, but first, Mandy, I think you should sit down. You are looking quite pale."

Realizing that sitting down was probably a good idea, I put the waterproof bag containing the letter back into my raincoat. After I had put the bag away, Coral pulled me over to a chair and made me sit. The chair looked like it was made out of sea sponges, and it was surprisingly soft.

Sirena took a deep breath. "Alright, here goes nothing. The reason why King Neptune does not allow marriages between merfolk and humans is because of a war that broke out between merpeople and humans long ago."

"A long time ago during the reign of Queen Marielle, humans did actually know about mermaids, and we all lived in peace," said Melody as she joined in. "However, humans started to take us for granted and kept wanting more than what we could give them."

"When Queen Marielle refused, the humans became

angry and came after us sparking war. They vowed that if they couldn't have what they wanted, neither could we," stated Isla.

Melody joined back in, "In order to protect us, Queen Marielle ordered that all humans were to no longer know about mermaids and put a curse on them to not remember us, and all of us merpeople disappeared from sight."

"However," said Coral. "The curse didn't work fully. Humans still remembered pieces and parts, but because we disappeared out of their sight, what they remembered became fairy tales. Ever since then, marriages between the two have become illegal, and each mermaid who married a human was given a choice to either vow to give the human up or to be outlawed."

I quickly cut in, "But what if the merperson and human had a child? What was the half-mermaid supposed to do?"

Coral looked a little uncomfortable about the question, but thankfully, she answered it. "Each half-mermaid had a choice. They could either live on land or live in the ocean, and whatever they decided, they would lose the other half of them forever. Once they made a decision, that was it, no more legs, or no more tail."

I swallowed hard. I wasn't sure what kind of answer I was expecting but that was harsh. I couldn't imagine losing either my legs or tail now that I knew about it. How could they have decided? "That doesn't sound pleasant."

"Well, let me explain it better. If the half-mermaid decided to live on land, they did in fact lose their tail, but if they decided to live in the ocean, they were allowed to keep their legs as long as they didn't go on land. However, there have been exceptions for the half-mermaids to go on land, but the only way they could do that was if they were on a special assignment from the king or queen."

"Oh."

Sirena paused a second before she continued. "King Neptune has been the strictest when it comes to illegal marriages. Both the mermaid and human are supposed to be locked away for eternity, and if they had a child, the child was supposed to either become a slave for him or be put to death if they found out about mermaids along with anyone else who found out."

At this, my heart stopped, and I couldn't breathe. This was why I wasn't supposed to know about mermaids. I put not only myself, but also my friends in danger by being here.

I could see my friends trying to snap me out of my thoughts, but I couldn't focus. The only thing that kept me from spiraling more out of control was the house shaking. At first, I was terrified that I had lost control of my magic and it was shaking the house, but I quickly realized that the storm was becoming worse with thunder so loud that it was shaking the house.

Chapter Seventeen

"The storm's getting bad," I stated mentally setting off my worries for another time. "I should probably head home before the storm gets any worse than it is now."

"That's probably smart," Melody said.

"But, are you going to be mentally ok after what we just told you?" asked Coral. "Your life could be in danger at any given moment."

"I'll be fine," I said with a small smile. "It will just be another secret I have to keep, but will you all be ok? All of you are in danger because of me."

Honestly, I didn't know if I was going to be ok. This was a bigger secret than when I found out about my powers and being a half-mermaid. It was right up there with finding out about my parents, but I didn't want to worry my friends. I had already put them in danger. It would be wrong of me to have them worry about me when their lives are at risk as well.

"Well, if it ever gets to be too much, don't be afraid to tell us, ok?" stated Sirena. "We all knew the risks before we became friends with you."

Tears started to come into my eyes, but I quickly wiped them away. "Thank you, girls, but right now, I'll be fine. However, I'm not sure how to get home from here."

"Oh, we can take you back to the island," said Isla.

"That would be great."

I quickly changed out of Coral's clothes and gave her pearls back before we headed back up the tunnel to exit Coral's house. As soon as we swam out of her house, the atmosphere had completely changed from when we arrived. Hardly anyone was outside anymore. All the merpeople we had seen before had taken shelter in their homes.

The sea was rougher with currents fighting to pull us into the massive waves above us. As well as the massive waves, the sky was pitch black. It looked like the whole sky was a dark hole without an end in sight.

"Coral!" I heard someone exclaim. I wasn't sure who had called out her name, but Coral and the others seemed to recognize the voice.

"Mom! Is something wrong? You're back from work early today." Oh, so the voice came from Coral's mom. I turned in the direction to see Coral's mom fighting her way through the water to get to us. I did a double take for a second. It was like I was seeing double of Coral. Coral looked exactly like her mom except for the fact that her mom looked a little older.

"Nothing's wrong, sweetheart. My boss let us go home early today because of this awful storm, but what are you all doing out here? All of you should be safe inside your homes! Not swimming around in these conditions!"

"We were going to take Mandy home, Mom."

She looked at me for the first time. She didn't seem to notice that there was one more mermaid in the group. "Oh, I'm sorry, dear. I didn't see you there. You must be a new friend of Coral and the others."

"Yes ma'am. I became friends with them a couple of weeks ago."

"I haven't seen you around before. Are you new here?"

I wasn't sure how to answer. Yes, I was new, but I technically didn't live here, but thankfully, Sirena helped me out. "She's from the next town over, Mrs. Cove. Mandy was visiting us, and we were going to take her halfway home; that way, she could find her way back since she hasn't been here before."

"Well, in that case you are going to have quite the swim in these conditions. How about you girls call your dolphins, so you can swim better?"

"Oh, that would make it so much easier. Thanks for the suggestion."

"That's what I'm here for. Just make sure you all stay safe."

"We will, Mom." Coral hugged her mom quickly, and we all fought our way to the entrance of the town.

"What did your mom mean by calling your dolphins?"

"Oh, right, you don't know," said Isla. "When we turn sixteen, we get a dolphin that we help protect from humans, and in return, the dolphins help us out as well by allowing us to ride on their back."

"There's a special connection between a mermaid and a dolphin. We can call each other using our minds, which is our way of communicating and letting the other know when they need help," Melody stated. "In fact, it's kind of like a friendship between a human and a dog. It's just mermaid style."

"That is awesome! I can't believe you all have your

own dolphin!" I exclaimed.

Isla laughed. "It is pretty neat, isn't it?"

When the dolphins arrived, Coral turned toward me. "Mandy, you can ride with me on Misty. She's super sweet."

"Aw, she's so cute," I said.

Coral pulled me over to her dolphin, Misty, and showed me how to pet her as well as how to hold on to her fin, so I wouldn't fall off.

I expected Misty to feel slimy, but surprisingly she wasn't. Her skin on the top kind of felt hard, but at the same time it wasn't completely. It was just firm, and it felt smooth and almost like rubber as well.

Misty's skin underneath was once again not slimy, and it was kind of soft instead of hard like on top. It's a weird comparison, but it kind of felt like the outside of a stress reliever ball, which meant it also felt a little squishy.

After petting Misty for a little bit, everyone got ready, and the dolphins started swimming to the island.

We swam through the water with ease as the dolphins took us to our destination. It was definitely faster than how it would have been if we tried swimming against the currents ourselves, and I enjoyed every second of it. I never thought I'd get to see a dolphin up close, let alone ride one! "Thank you for the ride, Coral. I'll see you all again soon!" I exclaimed as I patted Misty on the head and slid off her back.

"Stay safe!" Melody called out to me, as I started my journey back to land.

Although the swim here was easy, the way back was not. The waves kept picking me up and tossing me back into the water, which made me swallow way too much sea water, and I would end up coughing out of control. The wind was whipping my hair around, which made me regret not putting my hair back into a bun after taking the pearls out, and the rain pelted me in the face as I swam to the shoreline.

I finally pulled myself out of the ocean onto the sand when lightning struck dangerously close to where I was standing. My hair stood up, and I immediately curled up into a ball on the sand to protect myself from any more lightning strikes.

"Amanda!" Someone called out to me, and I looked up to see Mr. Sniper hurrying over to me as fast as he could. He must have seen me from his bait and tackle shop, which wasn't too far from where I was, and I really hoped he didn't see me transform into a human. "Amanda! Are you alright? I saw the lightning strike and was afraid it had hit you."

"I'm alright," I stammered. "It didn't hit me, but it definitely scared me."

"What are you doing out in this storm? You should be safe at home."

"I was out with some friends," I said with a shrug. I couldn't quite tell him the complete truth, and that was the closest I could get to the truth without blatantly lying. But hey, at least it seemed like he didn't see me as a mermaid.

Mr. Sniper eyed me suspiciously but didn't question it. "If you say so. How about you come inside the shop out of this storm before you get struck by lightning?"

Getting out of the storm sounded like a great idea, but I wasn't sure if going with Mr. Sniper was.

Chapter Eighteen

Mr. Sniper saw my hesitance in going with him to his shop. "I promise that you'll be safe inside the shop, Amanda."

I still wasn't sure if going with him was a good idea, but in the worst-case scenario, I could use my magic to protect myself if the need arose. "Ok, I guess I can go with you then," I said reluctantly.

"I promise that I just want to help you out of this storm before something happens to you. Now, if you are ready, let's head to my shop before we are both struck by lightning."

Our progress was slow as we fought our way through the storm, over the sand dunes, and into the bait and tackle shop. I was already soaked from the ocean, but by the time we had arrived at Mr. Sniper's shop, we were both dripping wet. I don't think that there could have been any more water on us, and don't even get me started on my hair! It looked like I had been electrocuted by the wind!

Mr. Sniper held the door open for me. "Go on ahead to the back of the shop. There's a door in the back that will lead to my house. You can either go on to the house or stay at the back until I can get this door locked."

"Ok, thank you." I could hear Mr. Sniper wrestling with the wind over the door as I cautiously walked to the back of the shop. The shop looked old and a little rugged, but it still stood fairly strong against the raging wind outside.

When I arrived at the back of the shop, I saw a door that said "Staff Only", which I assumed was the door to his house that was attached to the shop since there was no other door, but to be safe, I stayed put and waited for Mr. Sniper. I didn't want to walk into a place I shouldn't be in and get in trouble with him after he graciously offered me a place out of the storm.

Not long after, I could hear his footsteps coming closer, which meant he must have gotten the door closed.

"Oh," he said in surprise as he entered the back of the shop. "I would've thought you had gone into the house already. I'm sorry to keep you waiting if you were waiting for me."

"It's fine. I just didn't want to go through the wrong door," I said as I followed Mr. Sniper into his house.

"I'm going to get us some towels to dry off. Make yourself at home."

Even though Mr. Sniper said I could make myself at home, I didn't move very far from the door. I was a little afraid to move anywhere else. Besides, I was dripping all over the floor and didn't want to get everything wet. Instead, I surveyed the house from where I stood. The house looked a little old as well, but it did have a homely touch to it. It was also a little bleak in places, but that was to be expected from Mr. Sniper.

Mr. Sniper came back carrying some towels, but it also looked like he had changed into dry clothes before he came back. "Here you go," he said as he handed me two towels. "You can use one to dry off with and the other one to keep yourself warm since you don't have any dry clothes."

"Thank you," I said as I graciously accepted the towels because the chill of the air and my soaked clothes were beginning to bother me.

"Ok, Amanda. How about we sit down and talk a little," he suggested as he led me to the small family room. I sat down on one couch while Mr. Sniper sat down on the one facing me. "Now, what were you really doing out in that storm?"

"Like I said earlier, I was just out with some friends and got caught in the storm." It was the closest thing I could get to the truth. If I told him the truth, he probably wouldn't believe me or think that I am a complete and total freak.

He eyed me suspiciously again. I could tell he didn't believe me. "If I were to say that I believed you, why were you at the beach then? I know for a fact that you and your friends were not at the beach in this weather, and I also know that walking on the beach is not the fastest way to your home."

I stayed completely silent. I didn't know what to say. Mr. Sniper caught onto my lie, but I didn't know how to get out of it without sounding like a complete weirdo.

"Amanda," he said softly. "Tell me the truth. I promise that I will believe you as long as it is the truth."

I took a deep breath and sighed. There was no way I could get out of this. All my options have been thrown out the window. Why did he have to be so good at figuring out lies?

As I looked into his eyes trying to find a way out, I saw someone who cared about me. Mr. Sniper had looked out for me for as long as I could remember even though I was terrified of him. If there was anyone that might understand and not think of me as a freak, it was Mr. Sniper. "Fine, I'll tell you, but please promise me that you won't tell anyone about what I'm going to tell you."

"I promise."

"Alright, here goes nothing then. I'm part mermaid, which means that I may or may not have been out in the ocean with my mermaid friends. I know it sounds ridiculous, but it is really true."

Once I had finished, I knew there was no going back. Mr. Sniper now knows one of my secrets, and it was up to him if he kept his promise or not. However, I did feel slightly relieved to get it off my chest and finally tell someone besides my friends, but at the same time, I was terrified of what Mr. Sniper was going to say.

I watched Mr. Sniper carefully trying to figure out his thoughts as I waited for him to say something. Surprisingly though, he didn't look surprised and was eerily calm, which may have scared me more. Who would be calm when the person in front of them is telling you that they are part mermaid? Shouldn't he be freaking out right now?

"Amanda," he said softly. I held my breath waiting to hear what he was going to say. "I'm glad you told me the truth, but I already knew that you were a half-mermaid."

I was shocked. "What? How?" How was this possible? I always made sure no one was around when I entered and exited the ocean, except for one time. Did he see me exit the ocean not too long ago? That would make sense why he found me so quickly.

I heard him sigh. "I should've told you this a long time ago, but I was afraid you wouldn't believe me. I have known far longer about you being part mermaid than you have known yourself because- because Amanda, I am your uncle."

Chapter Nineteen

"Uncle? What do you mean uncle?" I cried. I was completely shocked. How was he my uncle and why didn't he tell me before?

"It's sort of a long story, but to begin with, I am your mother's older brother. However, before I go any further, I assume you found the pink box that I hid in your room behind your jewelry box?" Mr. Sniper asked.

"Um, yes, but what do you mean you're my mom's older brother? She didn't mention that in her letter, and not to even mention, how did you get into my room? Not only that, how did you even know about the loose panel in my closet?" I was slowly beginning to lose it. I had too many questions going on in my head and not enough answers. This was turning out to be a very interesting day, and I wasn't sure if I liked it or not.

"I know you are upset but hold on. One question at a time."

"Sorry. Guess I'm a little overwhelmed today."

"It's ok. I know it's a lot to take in, but if you will listen, I'll tell you what you need to know." I nodded and sat there quietly, patiently waiting for him to start. "Ok, after you were born, King Neptune found out about your parents' illegal marriage and came after them. However, your parents already knew that it was only a matter of time before King Neptune found out about them, so they were prepared." Mr. Sniper stopped his story and asked, "Are you still following?"

"Yes, I already learned about that from the letter Mom wrote to me."

"Good, just wanted to make sure. Anyways, they didn't want to leave you totally abandoned with two of King Neptune's half-mermaid employees, so your mom asked your father to manipulate her memories to bury the ones she had of me far away in her mind. That way, King Neptune wouldn't find out about me, and I could be here to protect you."

"Wait," I said, interrupting him. "How did Dad manipulate Mom's memories?" I was curious to know if Mr. Sniper knew about my magic. Plus, I was a little afraid about me having the possible ability to manipulate people's minds, which I don't think I wanted to have.

"There are special merpeople close to King Neptune who can manipulate memories by burying them or completely taking away pieces and parts of memories. I'm not sure how they do it, but it has something to do with King Neptune's trident. I heard from your father once that it is a very tiring process and sometimes deadly, which is the reason why King Neptune has merpeople do it for him."

Phew, thankfully, it sounds like I do not have that power, which gave me some relief. "So, Dad was close to

King Neptune, but he still married Mom?"

"Yes, your father loved your mother very much and said that it was a risk he was willing to take. As well as manipulating your mother's memories, your father also manipulated the memories of my parents to bury their memories of me as well to keep you safe."

"Wait, your parents, does that mean I have grandparents? Are they still alive? I just always thought that they had died since I've never seen them, and Mom didn't mention them in her letter."

"Yes, your grandparents are still alive. In fact, you have met them before. You just didn't know."

"Who are they? Are they someone I know well?" I started running a list of people that could be my grandparents through my mind, but I wasn't sure who it could be. There were too many options that might be potential candidates.

Mr. Sniper smiled. "Yes, you know them pretty well."

"Who?"

"In fact, you went to see your grandmother on Monday after you ran into me that morning, and you saw both your grandmother and grandfather that night."

I racked my brain trying to think of where I went Monday besides school. Then it suddenly dawned on me. "Oh! Is it Mrs. June, who runs the fashion boutique in town, and her husband Mr. Dan?"

Mr. Sniper nodded his head. "There you go. You figured it out!"

That was great news to hear. I was happy that Mrs. June and Mr. Dan were my grandparents. They have always treated me like their granddaughter since I was little. "I'm actually happy to know that. Wait, how did you know I went to the fashion boutique?"

"I'm sure you are happy. They were very adamant

that they would be able to still be like grandparents to you even after King Neptune had their memories of mermaids and you manipulated. It turns out that they were right, and to answer your question, I went there later to pick up some mended clothes your grandmother had sewed for me, and she was talking about what a kind young daughter you were to pick up thread for your mom."

"Oh, well I'm glad grandmother thinks of me like that, but why didn't they just keep their memories and have dad manipulate mom's memories of them?"

"Because, like I said earlier, they were positive that they could look after you even with their memories manipulated. Besides they didn't want to have to live with the thought of their daughter not remembering them. Believe me, I know how that feels. It's not fun."

It suddenly dawned on me why Mr. Sniper always seemed to be sad and lost in thought when I saw him. He not only had his little sister taken away, he was also forgotten by his entire family just to protect me. I also realized that he wasn't scary. He just wanted to look out for me. "Mr. Sniper, I'm sorry that you have had to live with the fact of being forgotten just to protect me."

"Please, call me Uncle James, and there's nothing to be sorry about. It's not your fault."

"But it is my fault. If you didn't have to protect me, you would still be remembered." I felt awful. It was all my fault.

Uncle James kneeled in front of me and looked at me dead in the eyes. "Amanda, listen to me. It was not your fault. Once I found out that your father could manipulate memories, I was the one who suggested it. Just like your mother, I didn't want to leave you unprotected. You are my niece. I'd do anything to protect you. Do you understand?" I nodded because I was too overwhelmed and couldn't speak. "Good," he said as he sat back down on the couch. "Now that that's settled, do you believe me?"

I wasn't sure what to believe, but the fact that he knew all of this about my family and mermaids, it couldn't have been a coincidence. "Yes, I believe you."

Chapter Twenty

Mr. Sniper- I mean Uncle James- broke out into a smile. "I am so happy that you believe me. You have no idea how much I wanted to tell you before but couldn't since it might've put you in danger. Again, I am so sorry that I kept all this from you."

Uncle James genuinely looked sorry, and I couldn't help but forgive him. He was family after all, and it wasn't like it was his choice. "It's ok. I understand why you had to keep it a secret." Before I could say anything else, my stomach growled.

"You must be hungry. I'll make us some lunch," Uncle James stated.

"Oh no, it's fine. I don't want to trouble you."

"Nonsense, it's no trouble at all!" Uncle James stood up and headed to the kitchen before I could protest further. "I'm afraid I do not have much, but will a grilled cheese sandwich and chips be alright?"

"That's fine. I'm not a picky eater most of the time." I followed Uncle James to the kitchen and watched him make lunch when I realized that he never answered a couple of my questions. "Uncle James?"

"Yes?" he asked, not looking up from the stove.

"You never answered my questions about why Mom didn't tell me I had an uncle in her letter and how you hid the box in my room."

"Oh, right. Well, about the letter, your mom didn't want to completely overwhelm you at one time, which is why she left out the fact that you had an uncle. As for how I hid the box, that's a story for another time."

"Ok." I thought it was weird that Uncle James wasn't telling me how he hid the box in my room, but I let it slide. I didn't want to push him too much, but suddenly, I thought of another question. "I've got one more question."

"What's that?"

"Why doesn't anyone know about my grandparents or you? Surely someone would remember that I'm related to you, Mrs. June, and Mr. Dan."

This time Uncle James looked up from the stove and turned to look at me. I must have caught his attention.

"I'm sorry, Amanda, but I'm afraid that I do not know the answer to your question."

"What do you mean?"

"I do not know why no one remembers. I'm pretty sure that your dad didn't erase them though. Oh, wait, I do know why no one remembers I'm your uncle. Your dad did do a nationwide memory manipulation on everyone who ever knew I was related to your mom and grandparents. I'm assuming Neptune did something similar about your grandparents. Sorry, I completely forgot about all that."

"It's ok, but uh, the sandwiches are-"

"Burning! Can't believe I forgot about the sandwiches!" Uncle James cried as he went to work trying to salvage them.

"I don't understand though. Didn't you say that it was dangerous to manipulate memories?" I asked, watching Uncle James scrap the grilled cheese sandwiches and start over.

"Yes, I did."

"Then why would Dad risk his life to do a nationwide memory manipulation? Wouldn't that have basically killed him?"

He looked up from the pan for a second to meet my eyes before looking back down. "It did almost kill him. He was extremely pale and collapsed after he had finished. He almost stopped breathing."

I gasped, covering my mouth with my hand. "Then why would he do that? Couldn't you have told the town that they had amnesia or something?"

"I'm afraid it would have been hard to convince everyone that they had a big enough accident to cause amnesia. Not to mention, word might have gotten back to Neptune that I was related to you. We couldn't risk it."

"But he could have died!"

"I know, but he knew the risks and did it anyway."

"But-"

"No, Amanda, there wasn't another way to protect you. He did it because he loves you."

"I know, but it still makes me feel bad that he had to go through all that just to save me."

Uncle James started pulling the sandwiches off the pan onto plates and looked at me. "Sometimes to protect the ones you love, you go to great lengths such as sacrificing your life, like your father, and sacrificing being remembered, like me. Wouldn't you do the same thing if you loved someone enough?"

I thought of Anthony and my friends. They would do anything to help me, and I would do anything to help them, even if it meant exposing my secrets, like I did when I saved my friends from the evil merman. I sacrificed keeping my magic a secret to protect them. "I guess so," I said reluctantly. I still didn't enjoy the fact that everyone was sacrificing things just to protect me, but what's done is done. I guess.

A couple minutes later, Uncle James set a plate down with my lunch on it in front of me. "Here you go. Eat up."

"Thank you."

We ate in silence, except for the storm raging outside, for a little bit until Uncle James broke the silence. "Amanda, I must confess that I know about your magic. I know that you may not want to talk about it, but I must ask you something."

So, he did know about my magic. He just played it off like he didn't. "What's your question? But before you ask, does that mean that Dad used his magic or Neptune's magic when he manipulated all of those memories?"

"Yes, he used his magic, not Neptune's. I wondered when you would ask that question."

"I knew it! I just didn't ask since I wasn't sure if you knew about my magic or not. Anyway, what did you want to ask me?" Great, that does mean that I have the power to manipulate memories, and I don't think I like that idea.

Uncle James cleared his throat and looked somewhat nervous. "I'm afraid to ask, but did you happen to go inside Moon Bay Cave?"

My mouth gaped open. How did he know about the cave? "How do you know about that cave?"

"Does that mean you did go inside the cave?"

"Yes, I went with my friends, but why does that matter?"

I watched as all the color drained from his face. "That's not good. This isn't good."

"What's wrong?" Uncle James was beginning to scare me now.

"Your mother told me before she was taken away that your father had brought you there as a baby to warn you to never go inside the cave because of a great danger inside. Your father hoped that if you were ever to find the cave you would have a feeling of uneasiness and not go in. He hoped that although the memory was forgotten, the feeling would stay."

I immediately remembered how I felt when my friends and I swam up to the cave, and as I remembered the uneasiness, I suddenly started to feel sick to my stomach. "What was the danger? Why shouldn't I have gone inside?" I was almost too afraid to know the answers.

"You shouldn't have gone inside because the cave was supposed to keep an evil merman trapped inside. The merman's name is Douglas. I don't know why Neptune decided to trap him in there, but whatever the reason was, it can't be good."

I could feel my heart start to race. The merman I had faced off with in the cave was Douglas. The impact of it all really started to set in. If I hadn't had my magic to protect me and my friends, none of us would be here today. "How do you know about Douglas?" I managed to ask.

"After your father had brought you to the cave, he told me just enough about Douglas, so I could understand a little bit about the danger you would be in if you went inside."

Uncle James had stopped talking and looked at me with fear in his eyes. He looked absolutely terrified, which made me scared. "What kind of danger am I in?"

It took him a second to answer, but when he did, I could've sworn my heart stopped beating for a second. "He's after your magic."

"What?" I cried as I jumped out of my chair.

Uncle James stood up and put his hands on my shoulders to keep me from doing anything rash. "Douglas' family has been after your family's magic for years, and these storms are most likely created by him to draw you out. He knows who you are and wants to finally take your magic."

I tried to pull away, but Uncle James kept me in place. I couldn't think straight. "Why does he want my magic?"

"I don't know." The house and shop started shaking, which cut off the rest of his thoughts.

We both looked at each other as if we were both reading each other's thoughts. We were both scared that it was Douglas coming after me. We ran through the house to the shop, which was shaking worse than the house, and looked out the front windows.

The storm was still raging, but the ocean had started to bubble up above the shoreline.

Chapter Twenty-One

Uncle James and I continued to watch as the bubbles started to swirl in a circle, taking my fears along with it. As soon as it began, the bubbles stopped foaming and the house and shop stopped shaking. When the bubbles completely calmed down, a chariot made out of a huge clam shell rose out of the water carrying a merman.

A merman had just appeared out of nowhere. I stood in shock, but at the same time, I wanted to run away as far as I could in case it was Douglas. It didn't look like the merman from the cave, but at the same time, I couldn't help but fear that it was him.

However, it seemed that was not the case. "Neptune," Uncle James whispered.

I turned to face Uncle James. "That's Neptune? How do you know it's not Douglas?"

"Because I was there when Neptune took your mother and father away. I was hidden so Neptune couldn't see me, but I could see him clearly."

"Oh." I turned back to the window to see Neptune's trident glow. Before I could wonder why his trident was glowing, a voice called out to me. "*Amanda*."

I turned again to Uncle James. "Did you say something?"

"No, is everything ok?"

"I could've sworn I heard someone call-"

"*Amanda, come here!*" the voice commanded.

"There it is again!"

Uncle James turned to look at me. "It must be Neptune. He's trying to call out to you by using his trident."

"*I know you are here somewhere, child. You better come now before I lose my patience!*"

My face turned pale. "What?" Uncle James asked. "What does he want?"

"He wants me to go to him."

"Then you need to go before he gets angry. I'll be right here watching you."

"I can't face him!"

"You'll have to eventually. It's better to face him now when he's not completely angry than when he is fully angry."

"But-"

"No buts," Uncle James stated as he nudged me to the door. "I'll be right here."

I sighed. There was no way I could get out of this. Although I could use magic to get away, I'd eventually be found. "Ok," I said half-heartedly as I walked out the door.

As I struggled through the wind and rain to reach Neptune, I got a better chance to see what he looked like. His hair and beard were both long and gray, and his tail was a shade of dark green. On top of his head, he had a gold crown, which was adorned with jewels.

When I finally reached the shoreline, I noticed that the chariot was being pulled by dolphins in gold harnesses, but before I could inspect them further, Neptune spoke. "Finally. How dare you make me wait, child!"

"I'm sorry, Your Majesty," I said as I dipped into a small curtsy. I didn't have a skirt on, but I felt silly bowing. I wasn't sure if I looked any more graceful curtsying, but it made me feel better.

Neptune stroked his beard. "Hmm, since you greeted me respectfully, I will graciously forgive you for making me wait. However, I must know if you went into Moon Bay Cave because when I visited the cave today an evil merman named Douglas was nowhere to be found."

I had to remember to be formal with Neptune. It might be my only way to stay on his good side. "Yes, Your Majesty, I am afraid that I have."

"And how did you find the cave?" I could see the moment he became furious with me. His face contorted into a scowl, and honestly, I wanted to disappear.

No matter how badly I wanted to keep my friends safe, I knew that Neptune wouldn't take an answer from me about just happening to find it since it wasn't too close to Davenport. "I went with some of my mermaid friends, Your Majesty," I replied meekly. I just hoped that my friends would be safe.

"How dare you go into the cave. You should have never been able to find that cave, and you should have never even known that you are part mermaid!" yelled Neptune. With each passing second, he was becoming more and more angry with me.

Before Neptune could continue yelling at me, an arm wrapped around my shoulders protectively. "Your Majesty," Uncle James said. "I would appreciate it if you would stop yelling at my niece and calmly explain what's going on." Having Uncle James' arm wrapped around my shoulders gave me a little comfort. It wasn't much, but it gave me relief to know that I wasn't facing Neptune alone.

"And who are you to be calling her your niece?" Neptune asked shooting daggers at Uncle James.

"I am her uncle, also known as her mother's older brother."

Neptune laughed. It wasn't a nice laugh though. It was a laugh that sent chills running down my back. "Well, it seems you all managed to trick me. Under normal circumstances I wouldn't let you get away with this. However, now is not the time for that, but don't get me wrong. I will deal with you later."

Uncle James, seemingly not afraid of Neptune, asked, "What do you want with my niece?"

"I need her to defeat Douglas because the sleeping spell her father put on Douglas was broken as soon as Amanda went inside the cave. The spell only lasted as long as her father or any of his descendants who has his magic didn't go in, but because she did go inside, I need her to fight Douglas where his magic is strongest, which is at a hidden river called the Dark River."

"I will not allow you to put her in danger," stated Uncle James as he pulled me closer.

"It doesn't matter. If she doesn't defeat him, the storms will become worse, leaving disasters everywhere, making life harder for everyone until ultimately the world is destroyed."

I flinched at the mention of the world being destroyed, but neither me nor Uncle James dared say anything.

I watched as Neptune stroked his beard while studying us, which definitely made me want to squirm under his terrifying gaze. Eventually, he spoke again, "I'll tell you what. Since I need you- and just so you know this is a one time thing-, I will promise you that I will not kill you or anyone who knows that you are a half-mermaid and allow you to ask of me one thing you desire if and only if you successfully defeat Douglas. However, my offer only lasts as long as you willingly help me. If I have to make you, the deal is off."

"I don't want you put in danger, Amanda," Uncle James said. "But it's up to you to decide what you are going to do."

I was torn. I didn't want to live in a world where only storms raged, but I also didn't want to fight Douglas. However, it was my fault that Douglas awoke, and I am the only one who can stop him. It also didn't help that I really didn't have a choice. At least this way, hopefully my friends and Uncle James won't get hurt. Besides, that favor may come in handy, which is like a once in a lifetime opportunity. "Fine. I'll do it. I guess I can finally put my magic to some use."

Chapter Twenty-Two

"Good," Neptune replied. "Then I will see you here tomorrow at the same time." The next thing I knew, Neptune's trident started glowing again. The water started bubbling, and Neptune disappeared along with his clam shell chariot and dolphins.

"Well, that could've gone better," stated Uncle James as he watched the bubbles disappear back into the ocean.

"I guess." I was still shaking from the encounter and was already regretting my decision. Uncle James still had his arm wrapped around my shoulder, and I was grateful for the little comfort it gave me.

"Come on. I'll drop you off at home. You'll need good sleep tonight for tomorrow," he said as he guided me to his car.

I didn't speak a word on the way back home. The events of the day had all finally caught up to me, and I was exhausted.

The next morning when I woke up for church, I could just vaguely remember getting home last night, and the looks of concern on Neptune's employees' faces as Uncle James brought me to the door of my house. I was in a daze the entire time, and I couldn't even remember getting into bed. I could just barely remember hearing Uncle James say that he was going to pick me up after church.

I dragged myself out of bed reluctantly and got ready for church. I didn't really care what I looked like, so I just put on a simple light purple dress that had yellowish, goldish stars and flats and decided to keep my hair down after brushing it. Although I wouldn't be changing after church, I knew the dress and shoes wouldn't be a problem since I'd be a mermaid not long after. However, I wasn't really sure if the bottom half would disappear when I changed into a mermaid or if it would stay whole, but I figured that was a problem to deal with later.

As I was walking out of my room, I figured that I should put on my heart-key necklace. That way, if I lost control of my magic, hopefully it would help me contain it, which would probably be a good idea since I haven't really used my magic that often. I have kind of just been relying on luck up until this point. However, on the upside, at least the small, light pink gems go well with my dress.

When I walked downstairs and into the kitchen, I saw that Neptune's employees had made breakfast for me.

"Hi, Amanda," the woman who I thought was my mother spoke. "We heard that you learned about everything yesterday."

Technically I found out about being a mermaid and the truth about my parents a while ago, but they didn't need to know that. "Yeah," I replied flatly, not really wanting to speak to them, but I had no other choice.

"We are truly sorry that you had to find out like this. Even though we were put here to keep you away from mermaids, we did want to protect you. We didn't want to see King Neptune take you away."

I didn't reply. I couldn't reply. I still didn't know what I thought of them, so I sat quietly eating my breakfast, hoping they would take the hint but of course they didn't or maybe they didn't care.

The man who I thought was my dad spoke, "Well, we understand why you aren't speaking to us, but we hope that you can forgive us in time. Since you know we aren't your parents, you can call us by our real names. I'm Irving."

"And I'm Maisie. For the record, we do truly love you. Over the years, we've come to think of you as our daughter. Not just some girl we had to take care of."

I still didn't want to speak to them, but I did have one question that I needed an answer to. "Why do you both look like my birth parents?"

Irving glanced at Maisie before replying, "Because your birth father changed how we looked with his magic before passing the magic to you. That way the people around town didn't think that your mother disappeared, and King Neptune wouldn't have to manipulate so many memories."

I tensed up and fought back the feeling of wanting to yell at them. They knew about my magic but never once mentioned it to me. They never once thought to help me with it either, which felt like a punch to my gut. "I should get going." I stood up from the table and walked to the door. I couldn't take it anymore. I had to get away from them before I did something I'd regret later.

"Good luck today, Amanda," Maisie called after me as

I walked out the door.

I fought with my emotions the entire walk to church. I was terrified of Douglas, mad at Maisie and Irving, and angry at myself for going into the cave. If I had never gone inside that stupid cave, none of this would be happening right now.

I was still processing my feelings when I walked into church and over to where I normally sit during the service.

Lost in thought, I didn't realize that Anthony had sat beside me. "Hey, Mandy, is everything ok? You don't look like yourself today."

"Oh, yeah, I'm fine." I couldn't tell him what was going on, but at least he cared enough to notice and ask me. Even though everything is changing, at least we are staying the same.

Anthony looked like he was going to reply, but the band started playing the music for worship, which took away his reply.

After the service, I got up to leave, but I remembered that Anthony and I were supposed to hang out today. "Oh, Anthony, I know we are supposed to be hanging out later, but something kind of came up. I should be finished with it by the time we were supposed to hang out, but if not, I'll text you. By the way, I'm so sorry to have to spring this on you."

"No problem, just let me know, and if we can't hang out, I'll see you tomorrow then."

I smiled, grateful that he understood. "Sounds good. I'll hopefully see you later today."

"Alright, but is this thing that came up the reason why you don't look like yourself today? I don't mean to pry, but all week you haven't seemed like your cheery self, and I'm kind of beginning to worry. Not to mention you were bouncing your leg throughout the service, which you only do when you're nervous."

"I'm sorry. I hope I didn't bother you. I didn't realize I was, but it's nothing, really. I've just had a long week. After some good rest, I should be fine."

Anthony didn't look convinced but let it slide. "Ok, but if you ever need to talk about something, don't be afraid to tell me."

"Ok, I will and thank you. I appreciate it," I said as I waved goodbye. However, I doubted that I'd ever be able to tell him. It would be too dangerous for not only him if he knew but also for me. Maybe one day if everything calms down, but I highly doubt it. I just hope that my secrets don't come back to haunt me later on or hurt our relationship.

Walking to the front of the church, I found Uncle James waiting for me at the door. "Hey, Amanda, are you all ready to go?" he asked.

"Ready as I'll ever be I guess," I responded as he guided me to where his car was parked, and we headed off to where we were supposed to meet Neptune.

While Uncle James was driving, he noticed I was wringing my hands and pulled the car over, so he could face me. "Amanda, do you want to talk about it? I noticed that you've been wringing your hands since we left church."

"Talk about what?" I asked, trying to feign innocence. I didn't want him to know how scared I was, so I focused on the rain pounding down on the windshield instead.

"You know, about Douglas." I opened my mouth to say I was fine, but he continued on. "Don't say 'you're fine' because I know you aren't."

"Fine, I guess I am scared of facing Douglas."

"I know you are, but the only way to get through it is

to face it head on and pray. You are an amazing girl, and I know that you will get through this."

"But what if I don't? What if I can't do it? What if Douglas wins, and everyone suffers because of it?" The dam had broken and all my fears had started to pour out before I could stop them. There was no way that I could do this.

"That's not going to happen. I believe- no, I know you can defeat him. Trust in God, and you can't go wrong." Uncle James reached for my hand and gave it a comforting squeeze. "Do you think you can face Douglas now?"

Even though I still didn't want to face Douglas, I couldn't let him remain free. Who knows what he would do. One way or the other I would eventually have to face him anyway. Might as well go ahead and get it over with. "I still don't want to, but I'll do my best."

"That's the brave girl I know," Uncle James stated as he smiled at me. "The sooner you defeat Douglas, the better you'll feel, and I promise that I will cheer you on every step of the way."

"Thank you, Uncle James. I don't know what I'd do if I didn't know you were my uncle."

I saw his lips curl into a small smile. "That's what I'm here for."

Chapter Twenty-Three

After Uncle James had helped me calm down some, he continued to drive us to the shoreline to meet Neptune. By the time we arrived, I could see Neptune waiting for us, and I could feel my nerves coming back.

"You are both late," Neptune stated. "And I do not like being kept waiting."

"I'm sorry, Your Majesty," I replied, dipping into a curtsy. "Uncle James was trying to help calm me down, so I could face Douglas."

Neptune asked Uncle James, "Is that right?"

"Yes, Your Majesty," answered Uncle James as he bowed respectfully.

"That is still no excuse for being late, but at least you weren't backing out of our deal, Amanda," stated Neptune. "Now, we must get going before Douglas makes these storms any worse. Amanda, you will swim in the ocean, and Mr. Sniper, you will be pulled along in a small rowboat by my dolphins. Let's go."

As Neptune's dolphins were pulling the rowboat over for Uncle James, I suddenly realized that I couldn't do this without the support of my friends. "Your Majesty?" I asked hesitantly. I wasn't sure if asking Neptune was a good idea or not. "Would it be ok if my mermaid friends joined us? It might help me focus better."

Neptune glared at me for daring to ask him a question. It looked like he was going to deny my request, but instead he sighed. "Very well then, if your friends will help you focus better, they may come if they want to."

"Oh, thank you, Your Majesty!"

"Now, where do these friends of yours live? I'll have my dolphins take a message to them and have them meet us over at the Dark River if they so choose to come."

"They live in Seadeep, Your Majesty, and their names are Coral Cove, Sirena and Isla Ray, and Melody Song."

Neptune nodded his head and beckoned some of his dolphins over to take the message to them. "Now then, shall we get started?"

"Yes, Your Majesty." I slowly entered the ocean since it was freezing from all the rain, but thankfully, it didn't take too long to adjust to the water after my tail appeared. I was also thankful that the bottom part of my dress disappeared with my legs. At least I wouldn't have to worry about getting tangled in it, and I had already left my shoes back in the car because who wants soggy, wet shoes.

Swimming to the Dark River was a challenge. The wind, waves, and rain were even stronger than they were yesterday. The waves pulled me under the surface multiple times, and Uncle James came very close to being thrown overboard as well as the boat being capsized.

By the time we reached our destination, I was already

exhausted. It took way too much energy swimming through all the raging waves. However, at least, Coral, Sirena, Isla, and Melody had also arrived, but they did look worried for me.

"Mandy!" Coral exclaimed.

"Are you ok?" Sirena asked, joining in.

"We saw the note," Isla added.

"What's going on?" Melody asked.

"Yes, I'm ok," I replied. I was a little overwhelmed by their reactions, but it was nice to see that they had come. "Remember the merman that tried to harm us at Moon Bay Cave? Apparently, he's after my magic, and I need to defeat him."

"Will you be ok to battle him?" asked Sirena.

"You've hardly used your magic, Mandy. Will you be able to control it enough?" asked Melody.

"I'm sure I'll be fine," I replied. "I hope. If things go wrong, I at least have my necklace to hopefully help."

"Also, who's that guy in the boat?" Isla asked, curiously.

"Oh, that's Uncle James."

"Uncle?"

"Apparently, he's my mom's older brother. I had no idea either. He just told me yesterday when he invited me into his house to get out of the rain."

"Ahem," Neptune said, clearing his throat, breaking off our conversation. "I believe we should get things moving. We don't have all day."

"Oh, yes, Your Majesty," I replied meekly. I really didn't want to begin, but I didn't have a choice at this point. "But where's the Dark River?" We were at the edge of the water where only huge boulders and trees could be seen. There was no river in sight.

"Because the river is dangerous, the Dark River can only be accessed after a secret hidden portal is activated.

That way no one can stumble upon it. However, Douglas and his family do not need the portal because their magic comes from the river, which means they can teleport to the river even if the river is behind the portal."

"That sounds so cool!" exclaimed Isla. I wasn't surprised she found this interesting. This was basically right up her alley.

"Oh, before I open the portal, Amanda," stated Neptune, "there are a couple things you must know. Only you can enter through the portal. Since Douglas' magic comes from the Dark River, it is too dangerous for anyone to enter except you until he is defeated."

"Oh, ok." I didn't exactly like that I was the only one that could enter, but there wasn't anything I could do about that.

"Next, I should warn you that both Douglas and the river can take your fears and worst nightmares and turn them into a reality. If you allow yourself to be swallowed by your fears or if you use too much of your powers, you could potentially die. So, make sure you keep that in mind."

"I'm not exactly sure I like that," stated Uncle James.

"Me neither," I agreed. I could feel myself start to shake as I let what Neptune said sink in. If I wasn't careful, I could die, which meant I probably had a fifty percent chance of surviving, if that.

Neptune spoke up again. "One last thing- wait for Douglas to strike first. By allowing him to, you can save more energy and hopefully drain Douglas' energy faster. Now, if you don't have any questions, I will open the portal."

I shook my head 'no', and I watched as Neptune commanded his dolphins to pull his chariot closer to the huge boulders.

Neptune raised his trident, and it started to glow. Just at the level of Neptune's eyes, three small holes appeared in the boulder in front of Neptune. Neptune put his trident into the three holes and turned it. As soon as he turned his trident, the boulder lit up brightly, and after the light disappeared, a soft blue colored river, which ran deep into the forest, appeared in the boulder's place.

"The portal is open. When you are ready, Amanda, you may enter, but please do not take too long. We must get this over with as soon as possible," Neptune stated.

I could feel my stomach twisting in knots. "I'm as ready as I'll ever be."

Before I could swim away, Uncle James pulled me into a tight hug and whispered, "You will do great. I believe in you."

As I was swimming to the Dark River, I could hear my friends yelling after me to stay safe and wishing me good luck. I really hoped that I would see them and Uncle James again.

However, right before I got to the portal, Neptune called after me as his dolphins pulled him closer to me. "Amanda, I forgot to tell you how your magic works. That way you have a higher chance of winning. You probably already know that your magic works when you imagine something, but that doesn't mean you can create something out of nothing."

"What do you mean, Your Majesty?" I asked completely confused.

"It means that to be able to use your magic you not only have to imagine what you want but you also have to be able to create it from something that already exists. Whenever your magic is used, it uses what's around to create it, which could mean wood, air, or in some cases, the owner's energy. When the owner's energy is used, the magic is at its strongest, but it also comes with a price. If too much energy is used, it will make you feel weak and incapable of moving, ultimately leading to death. So, be careful how you use it. Does that make sense?"

I gulped. The more I learned about my magic, the more I was afraid of using it. "I understand."

"Good, then carry on," he said as he was pulled back over to where everyone else was waiting.

I turned back to the portal, took a deep breath before entering into the Dark River, and as soon as I did, I realized that the atmosphere felt the same as when I was in Moon Bay Cave. It was cold and somehow eerie, which gave me chills and frightened me. The horrible memories of that day resurfaced, leaving me more afraid than before.

I had only swam a little bit into the river when the water started swirling up ahead of me, and my stomach turned along with it.

Chapter Twenty-Four

I mentally prepared myself as I watched Douglas appear through the swirling water. It looked just like how Neptune rose out of the bubbling water but definitely more frightening.

Memories of Douglas attacking me and my friends at Moon Bay Cave returned, which was not helping to settle my nerves. To make things worse, since he was in his element, he looked more terrifying than before. Even his fiery red hair looked like it was on fire, which added to his appearance.

For a second, all Douglas did was stare at me, and it felt like I was in a courtroom being stared down by the judge. Not that I've ever been in a courtroom, but that's what I imagined it to be like. Anyway, he was probably sizing me up to see how hard it was going to be to completely destroy me, and honestly, it probably wouldn't take much to obliterate me.

Before I completely lost my nerve, I saw his face contort into what I'm guessing was a smirk. Then Douglas laughed and pointed at me. "You are the one with the power to create things with their imagination?" Douglas asked, clutching his sides as he laughed. "You're nothing but a child. You can't defeat me."

Having Douglas mock me was not helping the situation. It was only adding to my fears. "How do you know I can't defeat you?" I asked quietly. I felt like a small, terrified child when they have to face a huge scary task.

Douglas was still laughing at me. "Trust me. I can snap you in two in no time."

Well, that was a lovely image to imagine. "Why do you even want my magic?" I desperately wanted to keep him distracted for as long as possible. That way I could maybe stand a chance of getting my fears under control. Even though Neptune wanted this to end as quickly as possible, I didn't want to lose the fight before it even started.

"Trying to distract me, I see."

Oh no, he caught on. He's going to be harder to distract than I thought. Maybe playing to his ego would work. "I was just wondering since I really don't know anything about you. I've hardly heard anything at all about you or your family."

For a second, all Douglas did was glare at me. Maybe I pushed him too far. "Well, I guess I need to educate you then, don't I?"

I shrugged. "If you want to." Yes, it was working!

"As you know, you have a great magical gift that was given to you. You have the power to create things with your imagination. My family was originally supposed to obtain that magic, but your family and someone else got it instead. Because of what your family stole from us, my ancestors became angry and searched for a way to get revenge and to take back the magic that was supposed to be ours. My ancestors found this river, which gave us our powers today, and now, it's finally time to take back what is rightfully mine!"

"*Amanda!*" Neptune called out to me telepathically, which almost made me flinch. "*What are you doing? Stop stalling!*"

"*I've got it under control, Your Majesty. I needed more time to control my fears.*"

"*Well, get on with it!*"

Douglas was done explaining, but he still wasn't attacking me yet. I wasn't sure how to get him to start attacking me like Neptune said.

However, I could faintly hear Uncle James and my friends cheering me on from where they were waiting, and I noticed that it seemed to agitate Douglas a little because his hands and eyes were starting to glow red. Douglas must not like that they were cheering me on, which gave me an idea.

"And how are you going to take my magic?" I asked Douglas, hoping that it would give me enough time to carry out my plan to figure out how to communicate telepathically with Neptune.

"My favorite question. The only way I can obtain your magic is when you are dead, which means I'm going to have to kill you first. Once you are dead, your magic will disperse into the atmosphere, and I can pull the magic into me, which will give me your powers," replied Douglas with a glint of glee in his eyes.

While Douglas was talking, he gave me just enough time to figure out how to talk to Neptune telepathically. I was able to somehow search the area with my mind, and connect to Neptune's trident, which gives Neptune the capability of speaking telepathically.

"*Your Majesty!*" I called out, finally connecting our minds.

"*What the- how are you able to reach out to me telepathically? You shouldn't be able to do that!*" Neptune replied, sounding baffled.

"*I'm not sure, Your Majesty.*" Being told that I shouldn't have been able to connect with him was definitely concerning, but I didn't have time to dwell on it. "*But I have a plan to get Douglas to start attacking. I need Uncle James and my friends to cheer me on as loud as possible. Douglas gets agitated when they cheer me on.*"

"*Alright then, I'll get them to cheer you on.*"

I severed the connection between me and Neptune right as Uncle James and my friends started cheering again, but this time, I could hear them better, which not only agitated Douglas, but it also gave me a boost of confidence.

Douglas' hands were turning bright red now. "Enough with the chit chat," stated Douglas. "It's time for you to go."

The next thing I knew, Douglas started firing balls of magic that definitely could have killed me, and I immediately started blocking the balls of magic.

Each magic ball that Douglas threw was bigger than the last, and he kept throwing them faster as time went on. All I could do was block them. I couldn't get a single ball of magic of my own thrown at him. He knew magic well, and I did not, which gave him the upper hand.

As time went on, I could feel my energy drain from my body, which meant my shields weren't as strong. It also didn't help that the rain seemed to be on Douglas' side because the rain kept pounding onto my shields wearing them down as well.

"Not as strong as you thought you were, I see. That will be your downfall," stated Douglas smugly.

When Douglas was talking, I thought I could hit him, so I lowered my shield, which was a mistake. He was waiting for it. As soon as I lowered my shield, Douglas attacked again.

I couldn't react fast enough, and his ball of magic slammed into me.

Chapter Twenty-Five

The force of Douglas' ball of magic sent me falling backwards into the river, as the ball of magic started to surround me. It was pulling me in, and fear and panic set in.

What was going to happen when Douglas' magic fully surrounded me? Will I die? If not, what will it do to me?

The last thing I remembered before Douglas' magic fully surrounded me was the cold water I crashed into and the screams of my uncle and friends as they watched the magic engulf me.

After the magic had fully swallowed me, I found myself in a black void. There was nothing to be seen for miles in any direction, and the air felt both cold and damp, which sent shivers across my arms. Wherever I was, it was not a place I wanted to stay.

However, the black void didn't last long. The darkness soon began taking shape. Colors flew past me as the darkness was being filled with something else.

The air was no longer just cold and damp. Something else was forming along with the colors that flew past me. I didn't know what it was, but the fear grew inside of me.

All of a sudden, the colors took shape, and I saw all of my fears and worries appear. Some were memories, and others were scenarios that I had created in my head. However, each one, whether it was a memory or not, created a sense of panic that grew within me as I watched each one.

I continued to watch each memory and scenario with each one creating more fear than the last, but eventually, I heard the sound of a child's laughter, which stopped me in my tracks. Why was there laughter in a place full of fear and heartache?

I wandered through the darkness following the sound of laughter. The farther I walked, the fewer memories and scenarios filled the darkness.

I continued to walk deeper searching for the laughter. The air was now chilly and blowing against me, which created goosebumps, but the laughter was ringing in my ears. I had to know what it was, so I pressed on braving the cold and fear.

The sound of a child's laughter continued to grow, and I found myself staring at a memory that I had forgotten. I didn't recognize it, but from the looks of it, I was maybe about six years old.

"Mandy!" a little girl with curly blond hair exclaimed with laughter in her voice. "Do it again!"

I started laughing, made a screeching bird noise, and jumped off a rock before landing on the ground and rolling. I looked like I was having a lot of fun, but what did this memory make me fear? I couldn't see anything wrong with it.

"Again! Again!" the little girl exclaimed. She looked to be about four years old, but full of laughter and happiness as she watched me act like a bird before falling to the ground.

I continued to act like a bird until I made a mistake. My foot slipped while I was jumping off the rock, and I crashed to the ground but not before hitting my head on the rock and landing on my leg awkwardly, which definitely broke it.

I screamed and felt myself losing control of my magic. Before I knew what was happening, I had unleashed my magic onto the little girl, which made her scream in pain as well.

"Mandy! Please stop! It hurts!"

"Luna!" I cried out. I didn't want to hurt her, but I didn't know how to stop. The pain had overridden my senses, and I couldn't control my magic.

The screaming had brought Irving and Maisie running out of the house toward us. They saw what was going on, and Maisie turned and ran back into the house while Irving was trying to calm both of us down.

When Maisie returned, she was holding my heart-shaped key necklace and managed to get it around my neck, and as soon as the necklace was put around my neck, it lit up and started to control my magic, bringing it under control.

Both Luna and I had stopped screaming, but Luna looked really pale and wasn't moving. I watched as Irving picked Luna up as fast as possible and rushed her to the hospital, while Maisie stayed with me and called an ambulance since she didn't want to move me for fear of a head injury.

As the memory faded, I sank onto my knees, remembering what I had just watched, with tears streaming down my face. Who was that little girl, and when did that all happen?

No matter how hard I tried, I couldn't place the memory, which was very frustrating, but the guilt of hurting her was enough to make me tremble. I had lost control of my magic and hurt an innocent child.

However, before I could dwell on the forgotten memory much longer, the black void started changing again, showing me another memory I had forgotten. There was no choice but to sit there and watch what I would guess would be another memory that would shake me.

I walked into the kitchen with a cast on my leg, but Maisie and Irving didn't seem to notice that I was there. They were talking quietly to each other, but I could hear every word they said.

"I don't want to send Luna away to your parents' home," Maisie said while sniffling.

Irving walked up to Maisie and pulled her into a comforting hug. "I know," stated Irving. "But that's the best way to keep both her and Amanda safe. We can't keep both of them here, and we can't send Amanda away since we are supposed to keep her away from everything."

"I know, I know. I love Amanda as if she was my own, but I also can't just give up my own child as well."

"We can't keep her here though. You know that. If something like that happens again, we might end up losing not just one of them but both of them, and you know that the future of mermaids depends on Amanda, even if King Neptune wants to deny it."

As soon as I heard they were sending Luna away, I walked back to my room as fast as I could on crutches and curled up on my bed. I was the reason why Luna was leaving, and I am causing Maisie and Irving grief over losing their child. If only I didn't have magic, I wouldn't cause harm or grief to anyone.

The memory once again faded, and I came to my senses. I had found the root of my fears. I didn't want to hurt anyone again, which caused me to fear my magic.

I wanted to give up and let Douglas win. That way, I could never hurt anyone ever again. I would stay in this darkness watching the forgotten memories over and over again to remind myself of what I did, if I had to. However, in the distance, I could still hear Uncle James and my friends cheering me on, hoping that I was still alive. Because of their cheering, I found a new resolve. I might be afraid to hurt someone, but I couldn't give up on the people who believed in me. They were counting on me to defeat Douglas, and no amount of fear was going to stop me.

As soon as I had decided not to give up, I felt something different. It felt like something had snapped deep inside me, and in its wake, a new power awakened in me.

Chapter Twenty-Six

The new, stronger power took over, and my fears faded away. I had found the root of my problems, and I could beat it. Uncle James and my friends aren't afraid of me. I wouldn't let my fears get the best of me, and I won't allow my fears to prevent me from keeping the ones I love safe.

As soon as I acknowledged my fears and told myself that I wouldn't allow them to control me, my full powers surged through me. I could feel my hands glow and my hair flow through the air as I overcame Douglas' spell.

As the spell broke, I could see Douglas and the river again, and I could also see Douglas treading water, in shock. He did not seem to expect me to break his spell.

Douglas could've also been partly shocked because I was floating just above the water, which meant that my tail had disappeared.

"You're a half-mermaid?" exclaimed Douglas. "How is that possible?"

I didn't reply. He didn't need to know, and I was focused on trying to defeat him. I wasn't sure how, but I knew that I needed to trap him first. That way, he couldn't escape from my grasp.

Then, I thought of it. I could trap him with a magical rope that he can't break. I floated closer to him, getting ready to trap him, but he noticed I was getting ready to attack.

His hands turned red with another one of his magic balls. "No, you don't get to attack me," Douglas said as he threw his ball of magic.

With my stronger power, I was easily able to stop the attack with a flick of my wrist, which scared Douglas. He started swimming backwards to put distance between us, but before he could get far enough away, I threw my magical rope around him and made sure that it was tight.

As soon as I had subdued Douglas, he looked at me and pleaded, "Please don't hurt me."

His attitude sure did change quickly. "Oh, I'm not going to hurt you, but I am going to take away your magic and the river's magic."

"What? Please, no, don't do that! Anything but that! You can hurt me. Just don't take my magic away!"

I didn't answer and started finding a way to get to the Dark River's magic source.

I searched by using the same technique I used to talk telepathically with Neptune.

I could hear Douglas' pleas, but I kept searching. My mind wandered until I found a trail of warm magic. I couldn't see it, but I could feel it. I followed the trail until I found a huge crystal buried in the rocks of the river, which carried the magic source.

I reached out to the crystal with my magic and pulled the magic into a jar that couldn't be broken or opened as soon as I closed the lid. Once the magic was safely stored away, I headed back to Douglas to drain his magic as well.

Finding Douglas' magic source was easier. It was stored in the back of his mind, and I drained his magic as well and put it in the jar with the river's magic source, meaning that both the river and Douglas had become powerless and could never use magic again.

"*Good job, Amanda. My guards will be there to take Douglas away in just a second,*" Neptune stated telepathically.

"*Ok, that sounds good,*" I replied, but I could feel my extra strength slipping away. I was becoming very lightheaded, and my whole body felt both heavy and on fire at the same time.

I had used too much of my energy by creating the rope and jar and draining the magic from the river and Douglas.

The last of my extra strength faded, and I crashed into the shallow water below me. I couldn't move, and I could feel myself losing consciousness.

Right before I blacked out, I heard splashes in the water. "Amanda!" Uncle James called out. Uncle James had managed to get to me and was cradling me in his arms. I wanted to talk to him, but I couldn't get my mouth to move.

Uncle James kept calling out to me, but his voice got softer and softer as I went under.

The next thing I knew, I was lying in a bed surrounded by a bunch of beeping machines. My head felt like it had been smashed by a ton of bricks, but I carefully sat up to find that I was in a hospital room. Uncle James and Anthony were there with me.

"Mandy!" Anthony exclaimed as he grabbed my

shoulders to balance me, since I was swaying from the sudden head rush I had gotten from sitting up. "Are you ok?"

I tried to speak, but my mouth was too dry. "Here. Drink this," Uncle James said as he handed me a glass of water. "I'm going to alert the nurses."

I gratefully took the water, and my throat felt wonderful as the cold water went down. "How long have I been out?" I asked Anthony.

"You've been unconscious for three days. The doctors were beginning to wonder if you were ever going to wake up, but I'm glad you seem ok now."

Before I could respond, a nurse came in with Uncle James and started checking to see how I was doing. Uncle James waited outside, but Anthony had to leave and said that he would check on me again later.

Thankfully, the nurses and doctors declared I was fine, and I was allowed to go home the next day, which gave me a lot of time to think about what happened.

Apparently, Irving and Maisie had a daughter named Luna who was sent to live with Irving's parents, but how did I forget about her? Did they manipulate my memories of her and what had happened? I mean, I guess they probably did, but still, it seemed like we were pretty good friends. If they manipulated mine, would they also have manipulated Luna's?

I was still thinking things over when Anthony came back right before visiting hours were up. "Hi, Anthony."

"Hey, how are you feeling?" he asked as he pulled a chair up beside my bed.

"I'm feeling pretty good, just a little tired and sore." Using my full powers definitely took a toll on my body, and I guess the crash into the river left me a little banged up.

"I guess that's to be expected. Mr. Sniper did say that he saw you get knocked into some rocks by the wind. What were you even doing out in that kind of weather anyway?"

That was a pretty good cover-up by Uncle James because technically I did land on some rocks. "I'm sorry, Anthony. I really am, but I can't tell you that. I can tell you though that it had something to do with the thing I had to do."

He studied me for a little bit before answering. I guess he wasn't sure what to do. "Was it something you had to do for your parents?"

"Um, kind of." Technically, it was somewhat for my parents but ultimately for saving the world. "I'm really sorry, but that's all I can tell you." I couldn't bear to look him in the eye, so I looked down at my hands. Because if I did look him in the eye, I would've wanted to tell him everything, which I could not afford to do.

"Hey, it's ok. I understand. You don't have to feel guilty for not telling me something that you can't tell me."

Even though he said I shouldn't feel guilty, I still couldn't look at him, which he seemed to sense. So he grabbed one of my hands and rubbed his thumb over the back of my hand, patiently waiting for me to look at him.

After taking a couple deep breaths, I looked up at him, but tears quickly came into my eyes due to the guilt of me technically lying to him.

"What the- why are you crying?"

I tried wiping my tears away but that only made me cry more.

Anthony moved to sit on the edge of the bed to face me. "What's going on? Why are you crying?"

"Sorry, I guess it's been a long couple of weeks."

Everything I've learned since the beginning of the school year must have finally caught up to me. From learning about being a half-mermaid to learning about my parents must have been enough to finally make me break down, but to be fair, I haven't really had a lot of time to process it all.

Anthony held out his arms, and I gladly allowed him to hug me, as I continued to cry on his shoulder. "Everything's going to be ok, Mandy. I don't know what's going on, but I know you'll get through it. Ok? Just hang in there, and I'll be here for you when you need me."

I nodded my head, but I couldn't help but continue to cry. Once I start crying, it's hard for me to stop until I've completely cried myself out.

He kept holding me in his arms and rubbing my back to comfort me, waiting for me to finish, and I was thankful that he was here with me. I don't know how I would've gotten through all those years without him.

Once I had no more tears left to cry, Anthony studied me for a second. "Are you feeling better now?"

"Yes, thank you. I'm sorry that your shoulder is wet."

"Don't worry about it. I'm just glad you're feeling better now, but unfortunately, I should get going. Visiting hours are just about up, but I'll swing by your house tomorrow after school to visit you. Try to get some sleep, ok?"

"I'll try. Good night."

"Good night, Mandy. See you tomorrow."

"See you." As I watched him leave, I wondered what I did to get so lucky to have him as a boyfriend.

The next morning, I was discharged from the hospital, and Uncle James came to pick me up. It was a nice sunny day, compared to the stormy weather last week, but it felt nice and gave me a little encouragement that I did well defeating Douglas.

"Amanda," Uncle James said as he was driving me home. "Neptune wanted to speak with you about your one desire he promised to give you. If you are feeling up to it, you can go meet him now. He said that one of his dolphins would wait for you at the shoreline and bring him there when you arrive."

"Ok, let's do that. I already know what my wish is."

"I kind of figured you did," he said, as he glanced at me, which made me wonder if he could guess what my wish is. "Oh, right, Neptune said that Douglas is currently waiting for his trial. However, Neptune did say that Douglas will most likely be locked away for life. They just have to do a trial since it's customary."

I nodded my head. Thank goodness Douglas was going to be locked up. I never wanted to see him again, and I shuddered as the battle flashed through my mind.

Uncle James started to turn the car around and head back to his shop, so I could meet Neptune. Once the dolphin had seen that I was there, it headed to get Neptune, and I patiently waited for him to arrive.

"Hello, Amanda. It's good to see that you are awake. You had everyone worried when you passed out, but I'm guessing you are here for your one desire to be granted?" asked Neptune.

"Yes, Your Majesty," I replied. "My desire is for my birth parents to be returned to me. That way, we can all live together and be a family."

Neptune shifted uncomfortably in his chariot and didn't look me in the eye. "I'm sorry, Amanda. I wish that I could, but I am afraid that I can't grant your request."

Acknowledgments

I know y'all might be a little upset at me for ending the book on a cliffhanger because there's nothing worse than being left on a cliffhanger, but I had to do it. I'm sorry! I know cliffhangers are terrible when you are waiting for the next book, but I promise it will be worth the wait.

Until then, thank you for reading this far. I never imagined that one day people would be reading my stories, which is still kind of weird to think about, to be honest.

Anyway, I have to thank my mom for all of the encouragement and countless hours she spent helping me. She has probably spent almost as much time on this story reading through looking for errors as I have writing it.

As for my dad and sister, I have to thank them for all the questions they asked about the plot, even though they sometimes asked the same question multiple times throughout the course of putting this book together. Lol!

I also have to thank my best friend Samantha for her interest in my book back when it was just a dream of mine and not anywhere close to being written. She and a couple other friends of mine helped me come up with Becky's name and character, which was fun brainstorming ideas with them.

Without the help of my self-publisher Anna Christine Boulier and my editor Contessa, this book would not be in your hands today so I am very thankful for all their help and patience, especially since it took months for me to get back to them with everyday life getting in the way.

Last but certainly not least, I most definitely have to thank God for allowing this opportunity to happen. It was all through His grace that this book has become what it is today.

About the Author

Hannah has enjoyed reading all of her life, which mainly consists of fantasies and mysteries. At the age of 14 her dreams of becoming a writer began to form. However, It only started to come together during a writing course she took in college and after meeting a local author in Anna Christine Boulier Publishing. Besides writing, she enjoys being creative in producing jewelry items and sharing her creativity with others, with writing as an added avenue to share that creativity. She hopes to continue her creative side in becoming a graphic designer, as well as sharing the beloved stories she has created.

www.ingramcontent.com/pod-product-compliance
Lightning Source LLC
Chambersburg PA
CBHW060425260626
47161CB00005B/1788